DRAWING FROM THE VOID

DRAWING FROM THE VOID

KC FETCH

To my book stepmom, Amanda. Without your help, this would never have been completed.

To my wonderful husband, thank you for the endless support.

1

Becoming

I hate that cake," Ellie grumbled as her mother fussed over her pig-tail braids. *It's dry, and the frosting looks like sugar paste.* She swatted her mother's hand. "Stop, Mom! You're gonna scratch my mark off my head."

"You want me to get Mee-Maw to do it?"

Ellie stopped complaining at that threat. Mee-Maw was an even rougher brusher than her mom. Then again, her curly hair didn't play well with others.

With arms crossed over her chest, Ellie pouted. *Worst birthday ever.*

As annoyed as she was, she couldn't say what she was thinking out loud. For the last month, her parents had dedicated day and night to this event. Elijah, her father, mowed and painted, procured propane heaters, and warded off overstepping family members—not to mention patiently managing Mee-Maw. Ellie's mother, Kimberly, sent out invitations, collected responses, organized parking, and made food. And, of course, she also had to entertain Mee-Maw when the old woman wasn't breathing down Elijah's neck.

The guest list was the most egregious irritation of all. When Ellie had complained, Mee-Maw used the most pathetic tone she could muster. "At my age, you're lucky if you still have friends left." Everything that escaped Mee-Maw's mouth was coated in an extra-thick layer of guilt. With an overdramatic sulk, she lifted her frail hand. "What's a few more families? It's like you don't want me to be happy."

"No, no, Mother. We *do* want you to be happy," Ellie's mother had replied. "I can always just double or triple a recipe." Mother always caved to Mee-Maw.

"There we go." Her mom set the comb down on the end table. Satisfied with the braids in Ellie's hair, she invited her daughter to partake in her excitement. "Have a look at them."

"Seen one braid, you've seen 'em all. Am I free now?"

"Ellie-Lynne!"

Ellie groaned loudly and took the pocket mirror from her mother. Just like the last ones and the test runs before those, the tight braids started near the top of her head and trailed down behind her ears, where they dangled down to her shoulders. Her curly mahogany hair twisted up at the ends past the hair-tie.

"Yup, looks great. Can I go now?" Ellie held the pocket mirror over her shoulder for her mom to take it.

"Oh, fine." Kimberly patted Ellie on the back, and she took the opportunity to run. "Don't go far," her mother called out. "Mee-Maw wants to introduce you to some people."

Spotting Mee-Maw and her friends, Ellie froze in her tracks. The sea of awful, stuffy, weird people had already begun. They only wanted to talk about local politics, crops, and gossip. The latest chatter surrounded the marriage of Candice Hurst to her third cousin, Damien Branham-Hurst.

"Scandalous choice," a snub-nosed woman commented.

"Little too close in the gene pool if you ask me," Mee-Maw replied. She always looked so smug when gossiping. "That's why we have been reaching out to our Canadian brethren..."

Ugh. Ellie normally tuned out the conversations within the first thirty seconds, but tonight, there would be no use hiding. She was the center of attention, even if her hideous hand-me-down outfit didn't give her away. Ellie hated the loose, white blouse covered by a black sleeveless dress with green lacy fringe and matching green ribbons crisscrossing down her chest and abdomen. The revolting attire was complimented by a green apron and tight, uncomfortable black flats.

During her first fitting two months ago, Ellie had pleaded her case. "It's 2014," she whined as her mom took in the waist of the old garment. "Can't we let go of some traditions or maybe jazz it up? Like we could keep the shoes, but maybe I could wear a normal green dress?"

"You have the mark; you wear the dress," her mother had replied, poking her with a needle. "If you'd stop moving, that won't happen!"

Ellie's upper lip twitched at the memory. She had been dreading this day for weeks, but every witch and wizard blessed with a connection to the Void was celebrated on their fourteenth birthday. And unfortunately, boys and girls alike had to wear traditional German attire to honor the shores from which they came.

So hung up on tradition, but I'm the only one dressed like a clown.

Ellie had never even attended a Becoming Ceremony. She wanted to go to her cousin Lianne's party five years earlier, but her parents said that midnight was too late for children to be up, so the Becker house didn't attend. Mee-Maw had voiced her irritations during their weekly Friday night dinner. Ellie tried to block that memory out, too, but looking around, she realized her parents were right. It didn't seem like a child's affair.

She took a second to take in the scene. Black metal garden benches with decorative backs were lined up beneath propane tanks. Plush cushions lined the seats, and decorative end tables accompanied each bench. Twinkling lights extended up each propane lantern.

The guests dressed as if this was the event of the year. Some wore ties, and others wore blazers. She spotted her father's boss, Mr. Anderson. For the head of an accounting firm, he was bulky and intimidating in his black, heavy suit. Two men in identical bright orange windbreakers flanked Mr. Anderson. They had the same short haircut and matching tattoos of the letters "V" and "A" overlapping on the backs of their right hands.

Weird, Ellie thought.

***

The hours seemed to rush by in minutes as Ellie was introduced to dozens of new faces.

"Spitting image of her mother," one old man with a massive nose commented.

"Such sweet pigtails," a broom-thin woman added.

"Kimberly, she has your eyes." Ellie heard that one multiple times.

Other comments echoed around her. "Yes, she dresses up well, but describe the lady's demeanor."

"What magical ability has the Void gifted her with?"

"Is there other potential in the bloodline?"

Ellie would have given anything to speak with someone her own age, but Lianne was the only other young person here, and she was five years older than Ellie. Lianne grew up on her father's land in New Hampshire, so they didn't see one another often.

After the millionth introduction, Ellie hung over the armrest of a bench and played with a crunchy dead leaf that had dared to make its way onto their perfect lawn.

"Ellie-Lynne," Mee-Maw hissed and smacked Ellie's shin with her cane. Elijah swiftly took a firm grip on it, and then her father and grandmother held one another's gaze intently. She half expected her dad to yank the cane away from Mee-Maw and tell her to sit in the corner until she could behave.

"Your child has no manners," Mee-Maw snarled and tugged her cane back.

"Ellie, sit up, please," Elijah asked softly, but his eyes lingered on Mee-Maw.

"Can't say much for her attention span," Mrs. Klein added with puckered lips. She and her husband were Ellie's least favorite of Mee-Maw's friends this evening. Aside from her judgmental way of speaking, she was dull and had horrible taste in cake.

When Mrs. Klein took a dainty bite from a slice of Mee-Maw's double-chocolate raspberry cake, a smear of frosting remained on her top lip. Ellie suppressed a smile.

Somewhere around eleven thirty, Ellie managed to slip away to the food table. That double-chocolate cake loomed over everything else.

Yick. Her mom was an excellent baker, and everything she made was better than Mee-Maw's nasty cake. Ellie dunked a carrot in some creamy dip, and before she could take a bite, she felt a hand on her shoulder.

"Happy birthday, Ellie-Lynne," Megan, the golden child, cooed with a kiss on her cheek.

"Just Ellie," she reminded Megan for the millionth time and pulled away from the unwelcome kiss.

Of course, Megan was gorgeous in a flowing gown with shimmering silver sequins, which glimmered on her plump, pregnant belly. Tiny clips in her dark-brown hair added an extra layer of sparkle to the ensemble and the stylish updo.

"Number five?" Ellie asked and pointed at her cousin's stomach. It seemed like every time Ellie saw Megan, she was pregnant. There was a running joke between her parents that Megan and Cole were trying to build up an army along the Maine-Canadian border.

"Six," she corrected with a wide smile. "Think this will be it for us unless it's another girl. I want another little boy so bad."

"Good luck." Ellie didn't have the energy to hear Megan's baby stories. She turned away when her cousin grabbed her braids.

"You look so cute in your dirndl."

Ellie protectively pulled away. "Don't! If you mess my hair up, my mom will never leave me alone."

"Well, of course, she won't leave you alone. It's such a big day. Today's the first day you show the world you're a woman!"

"I'm fourteen," Ellie flatly reminded her.

"Exactly." With sparkling eyes, Megan glanced over at the gift table. Sure, there were a few boxes, but the table mostly held envelopes of varying sizes and thicknesses.

"Today's your Becoming Ceremony. Next, you'll get married, move out of your parents' house, and have children. It's so exciting." Megan's eyes glistened with distant memories. She chuckled softly before she looked back at Ellie. "My table was filled."

"Cool," Ellie commented without enthusiasm. "Modest as always," she muttered to herself as she turned away to grab another carrot. Just then, a large, delicate hand brushed against hers. "Oh, sorry." Ellie pulled her hand away from the vegetable tray.

"Oh, no, no, my apologies." A full, deep voice she didn't recognize reverberated across the table. Ellie looked up to see a young man with pale skin and dark-brown hair. "You're the birthday girl."

Obviously... I can't even get food without people wanting to talk my ears off. She felt the muscles in her jaw tighten.

"So well behaved at the veggie tray... probably can't wait to get into something sweet, right?" His lips curled in a manner that made Ellie's skin crawl.

Her face distorted with discomfort. *Weirdo.*

"Are you trying to tell me you don't want a piece of that cake? I've seen you eyeballing it." The stranger's tone dropped as he leaned over the table towards her. "We could steal a piece together. I won't tell anyone."

"No thanks." Ellie stepped away from the table. *No food's worth this.*

When her backside bumped into something firm, she jumped and turned around to see her father. His mustache was perfectly manicured, and his long hair was pulled back into a loose ponytail.

Oh, thank the Void.

Her father held a small plate loaded with Aunt Julie's taco dip and chips. "Careful, sweety."

"Sorry."

"You must be starving." While he spoke to her, his eyes locked onto the man across the table.

"Yeah, but he's weirding me out," Ellie whispered.

"Don't worry. I'll distract him." Elijah held out the plate to Ellie. "Go take a break; you've done a great job entertaining."

"Elijah, just the man I wanted to see," the creepy man's voice sounded behind Ellie.

The hairs on the back of her neck stood on end, so she took the plate, muttered a quick thanks, and backed away.

"Hello, Kevin." As Elijah assumed a formal, polite tone, Ellie made as much distance as she could.

With Mee-Maw's help, the garden was still in bloom on this chilly October evening, so Ellie sought solitude among the pumpkin leaves and overgrown collard greens. Crouched down above the chilly dirt, she took the biggest bite she could manage of the taco dip. Layers of juicy meat, creamy cheese, and smooth guacamole filled her mouth with each greedy bite. *So much better than carrots.* She sighed. *Finally alone.*

She watched the lazy crowd from her vegetable-shelter. The food table was along the backside of the cozy, off-white farmhouse. Out in the yard, the guests sat around the heaters, which Ellie missed the moment the first cold breeze swept through the garden.

While her father entertained the creepy man, her mom inspected the ritual area. From here, Ellie couldn't see the overlapping circles and symbols Kimberly fussed over.

As long as it's not my hair, Ellie thought as she took another bite of dip.

"Can you believe she openly admires Conrad like that? So disrespectful," a nearby voice rang out.

Ellie recognized the woman's voice from one of the first families Ellie was introduced to. This woman had pale blond hair, thin pink lips, and scrutinizing eyes that made Ellie feel two inches tall. Her husband was an older, plump man with thinning hair, a trimmed mustache, and thick eyebrows. Compared to her father's glorious mustache, it looked pathetic.

Ellie peeped around a collard bush to make sure they hadn't seen her.

"She needs to give up. There's no spot in Oren for her," Mr. Hurst added.

"Yep. Pamela needs to spend more time tending the crops rather than trying to get a rise out of him."

Both adults snickered. Ellie didn't get it.

"It's pathetic."

"Oh, how the mighty have fallen, my dear," Mrs. Hurst said, and they continued their pre-ceremony promenade along the edge of the garden.

Ellie had heard the word "Oren" a few times throughout her life, but she didn't know why anyone would need a spot there. From what she gathered, it was the place in Maine where they sent their excess vegetables, spices, and herbs. It was the reason her family had to maintain a small farm—and why Mee-Maw lived so close—to provide helping hands for multiple harvests.

Shamelessly, Ellie licked the plate clean before she emerged from her foliage shelter and returned to the party when she heard her mom asking for her.

"I was just taking a break," Ellie explained and placed her plate amongst the dirty dishes by the door. Kimberly had somehow kept the bussing area clean while entertaining, refilling drinks, and inspecting every other detail.

"And getting covered in mud," her mom fretted, cleaning Ellie's chin. "What green thing did you get into?"

"Guacamole," Ellie admitted.

Kimberly stopped fussing, took her daughter's cheeks in her hands, and looked down into her eyes with a caring expression. "Oh honey, we never stopped to grab you food. I'm sorry. Do you need a snack before the Showing and Unveiling?"

"Dad got me food." *Please don't touch my hair. Please don't touch my hair.*

Kimberly smiled thoughtfully, then gave her daughter a kiss on her forehead. "Do you think you'll be able to Channel the Void before everybody? Can I get you some Focus?"

"It might help," Ellie confessed. She had never meditated or channeled before a crowd.

"I'll grab you a spoonful." Her mom stepped past her to the backdoor, which was cleared away of dying vines and plants. The screen door creaked as she pulled it open, and Ellie saw her mom cringe at the sound.

"Mom?"

"Yes?" Kimberly stopped in the backdoor's light. She looked so pretty in her full-length, long-sleeved copper dress. Ellie was lucky to inherit her mother's bright blue eyes and button nose.

"Could I have it on an apple slice?" Ellie looked at her mom with pleading eyes. The focus potion was thick like peanut butter and hard to get down. Flavor-wise, the ginger and lemon balm fought for dominance, so the slice of apple helped to mellow it out.

"I was going to give it to you that way anyway." Kimberly smiled sweetly before she stepped inside the house.

Ellie nervously tugged and adjusted her attire. Though it was weird and she hated it, Ellie didn't want to look like a sloppy fool before everyone.

Her mom quickly returned through the squeaky door with a sliced, cored piece of apple smeared with the teal, thick potion.

"Thanks." Ellie shoved a portion of it into her mouth and quickly chewed.

Kimberly's pudgy fingers rubbed the bottom half of Ellie's face.

"Everyone!" Elijah's voice boomed from the ritual area. "Thank you for coming—"

"I'm so proud of you." Kimberly pulled her daughter into a hug and kissed her forehead.

Ellie tightly squeezed her back. *Come up there with me, Mama.* She buried her head into her mom's soft shoulder as nerves consumed her.

"My lovely daughter, Ellie-Lynne Betty Becker." Elijah gestured towards the house, and Kimberly turned Ellie around to face the crowd.

"Go on, now. Just be your wonderful self," her mom muttered and patted Ellie's lower back.

The dark stretch of grass to her father felt like miles of undiscovered, rough terrain. By the time she reached his side, sweat covered her forehead.

"Don't worry. Just remember the dandelion in the wind," he whispered to her as he gave her a loving hug.

Dandelion in the wind. Dandelion in the wind, Ellie repeated her dad's guided meditation she had heard since the first time she meditated as a small child.

Carefully, she stepped over the painted lines of the three small circles, representing different stages of the moon. An upside-down triangle was in the center of each moon, and in the center of it all was one hollow circle—the new moon. A tiny bouquet of white petaled flowers with yellow centers sat on the chair in the center circle. Ellie picked up the bouquet, took a seat, crossed her legs, and tried to ignore the sea of faces before her. Self-consciously, she tucked her dress between her legs to preserve her modesty.

Stupid zip-zaps. People came all the way here to see this?

With a shaky exhale, Ellie relaxed her head and placed her hands on her knees.

Dandelion in the wind.

She took another deep breath in and slowly counted to three as she exhaled. In her mind, she pictured the white puffy top of a dandelion seed as it drifted on the wind.

Dandelion.

The mark on the crown of her head grew warm as she felt the essence of the Void, the birthplace of magic, pour into her. A gentle tingle built up at the base of her spine and trickled down into her core. Every nerve in her limbs awakened with the sensation.

Ellie opened her eyes and brought her hands together without letting them touch. As she focused the tickle of the Void into her fingertips, bright white sparks danced between her digits, and then, an electric line formed. The line disappeared, and the electricity reappeared. She focused, allowing the zaps to click and clack back and forth.

How long do I keep this up?

Ellie glanced up from her hands to her father.

Elijah gently nodded and turned back to the crowd. "That concludes the Showing. Now, we shall begin the unveiling." He gestured towards the row of candles on the table.

Kimberly scurried to light them, but her plump frame could only move so quickly. As if to make a point, Mr. Anderson flicked his wrist, beckoning the candles to life.

"Thank you," Elijah said respectfully. "I'd like to invite the oldest living relatives to give their blessings. First, we'll have my mother-in-law, Pamela Keller-Wagner."

Mee-Maw stood tall with her salt-and-pepper hair. Her full-length, deep green dress ruffled in the breeze as she approached the candles and took one.

Ellie stood, bowed her head, and bent her knees so her grandmother could kiss her mark. Then, the old woman turned, blew out the candle, and took it to the empty table on the other side of the ritual space.

"Now my own father, Ralph Becker."

The frail old man with an open blazer that showed his striped button-up shirt and suspenders shuffled over with his candle and kissed Ellie's mark.

"Good job, kid," he whispered before he blew out his candle.

Next up was Grandma Edna Becker, a shy older woman with freshly curled silver hair and a petite but sturdy frame.

Following her parents, anyone in the crowd was welcome to approach and give their blessing. First in line was the creep from the veggie platter. As he took his candle and walked over to Ellie, her heart pounded in her ears. She didn't want him anywhere near her.

Dad, please. She looked at her father, standing near the end station with her grandparents and mom. Elijah stood tall and kept his eyes sternly on the man as he approached.

Just then, Megan screamed, "Look out!"

Everyone turned and followed her finger as she pointed towards the sky.

From the heavens, yellow, red, and blue flames danced and spiraled before they crashed through the heavy plastic table full of food. The smells of burned sugar and spicy barbecue sauce filled the air as the table collapsed, and all the food slid into the center.

The world stood still around them as the crowd watched on.

Finally, the flames subsided.

Then, the crowd gasped as they heard a harsh rhythmic banging sound against the side of the plastic table. Everyone strained to see, but only a shadow darkened the collapsed table.

Whispers filled the air.

Ellie took a step forward toward the mess.

"Ellie, don't!" Elijah rushed across the lawn in front of Ellie. He held out his left hand to shield her from the intruder.

Then, a long-eared, brown and white basset hound popped up out of the mess. With its saggy expression, it simultaneously looked young and distinguished.

A large glob of frosting sat on the top of its head. The hound's deep brown eyes found Ellie immediately.

"Hi," a silly, gruff voice chirped at her.

Did that dog just talk?

As its tail slapped loudly against the side of the table, Ellie returned its greeting with a wave and a grin.

It's so cute!

She wanted to wrap it in a big hug. It was the funniest creature she had ever seen. With clumsy feet, the basset hound wiggled out of the heap of food and hurried across the grass past the stunned Elijah. Upon reaching Ellie, the dog jumped into her awaiting arms, leaving cake, taco dip, and guacamole on her traditional garb. The hound nuzzled its wet nose against her cheek and licked her as its joyous whimpers filled the air.

Tears filled Ellie's eyes as she turned to her father. "Can I keep him?"

With wide eyes, Elijah nodded slowly.

"Everyone," Mee-Maw yelled, drawing the attention of the group as she approached the messy duo. "It appears that our Ellie-Lynne has been blessed with a Familiar!"

2

Bullfrogs

F ive years later, lush bushes surrounded the perimeter of the off-
white farmhouse. An unseasonable garden overflowed with flowers, herbs, and vegetables. Flat stepping rocks populated the main
path. Robins and chickadees filled the surrounding forest with a welcoming lullaby on that late spring morning.

"Guess who woke up first?" Ellie sang as she repositioned Louie's
large ear.

The half-awake basset hound stuck his tongue out, and Ellie covered his face with the opposite ear, mimicking the game of peek-a-boo.

"I get to annoy you," she continued.

With his sausage-like frame, Louie attempted to scootch forward
underneath the fluffy comforter.

"Are you trying to sneak up on me?" Ellie asked.

Louie's tail wagged beneath the covers. With a poorly executed
leap, Louie pushed her backward onto the bed.

"Help, help, I've been attacked by a hot dog!" Ellie laughed as the
chubby dog sat on her chest.

"I am *not* a hot dog! Take that back." The saggy-eared canine stood
over her with a determined glare. "Take it back, or I will lick your
face."

Ellie narrowed her eyes. "You wouldn't dare." With a large, wet tongue, Louie licked her cheek, and she squealed with laughter. "No! I won. I get to bug you. That's the rules."

"I follow nobody's rules," Louie declared and continued his attack.

"You're so full of crap," Ellie said as she wrapped him up like a burrito in the blanket. Louie whined and lay helplessly on the bed. "Admit defeat," Ellie demanded.

From down the hallway, her mother roared, "Stop playing with that dog! Make yourself useful and do some chores."

Ellie stuck her tongue out at the door. Even though Ellie was nineteen years old, her mother still liked to bark orders at her like she was a child.

"That dog," Ellie mocked before she turned back to her basset hound burrito.

Louie freed one paw from the top of the comforter. Ellie grabbed it and gave it a squeeze.

"I will get you for that," Louie threatened.

"Oh yeah, I'm sure." She pulled the blankets away from him. "Big talk for someone who can't escape a blanket wrap."

Louie rolled over onto his stomach. "I happen to like being swaddled like a baby, thank you." Louie hopped off of the bed and retrieved one of the smaller pillows Ellie had kicked off the bed during the night. He returned it back to its rightful place on the bed.

"Sounds like the kind of excuse someone who couldn't escape a blanket wrap would make." With his help, Ellie straightened the sheets.

"We both know I could've escaped if I wanted to," Louie countered as he stood up on his back paws and elongated his frame so he was as tall as she was.

Ellie put her hands up in defeat. "My apologies, sir." As she fixed the sheet, she added, "Still think you're a big baby."

Just then, Louie threw a sock at Ellie's head, but she dodged it.

"You'll have to be faster than that if you're going to surprise me, slinky-boy."

"What did you call me?" Louie asked.

Ellie slowly enunciated each word. "Slinky... boy."

"Oh, that's it," Louie replied, and he threw a pillow, which landed this time, hitting Ellie in the head.

Ellie shrieked with laughter. "I'm going to get you!"

"I swear to the Void, if you don't stop playing, I'll double your chores," Ellie's mom threatened from the other side of the door. At this point, Louie had Ellie trapped under a pile of dirty clothes from the hamper.

They both sighed with disappointment.

"She's a fun killer." Ellie pouted and begrudgingly cleaned up the mess.

It was a typical Thursday in the Becker house. Her dad, Elijah, was off at work at the accounting firm. In Ellie's words, he played with a calculator all day and talked about debits and balances. She liked to poke fun at him, but from spreadsheets to car engines, if there was a problem, her father would figure it out. Ellie and her mother would be helping Mee-Maw again today with her harvests for Oren, Maine.

"Dog! Get the branches out of the yard," Kimberly shouted from the kitchen like a drill sergeant.

Ellie's nose twitched as she scrubbed the grout off the bathroom floors and shouted back, "Stop ordering him around like that. He's my Familiar!"

"He lives in *my* house and eats *my* food," Kimberly shouted back.

"It's okay, Ellie. I don't mind." Louie picked up his scrub brush between his teeth and dropped it back into the bucket. "Besides, the branches are heavy. I don't want either of you hurting yourselves trying to lift them." With that, Louie disappeared from the bathroom. "I'm on it, Kimberly," he announced before the screen door to the backyard shut behind him.

She's always ordering him around. Ellie scrubbed harder at the floor. *She needs to back off. She's just jealous because she can't do any magic, while I got a gift and a Familiar.*

While Ellie scrubbed the bathroom floor until it sparkled, Louie dispatched of the offending branches. Then, they carried a jug of water and their gardening gloves down the old country road known as Azalea Way to Mee-Maw's farm.

Mee-Maw's house was a small pistachio-green cottage with a single-car garage. The no-frills yard lacked trees, playground equipment for the grandchildren, or even patio furniture. Instead, it was filled with rows and rows of plants.

Ellie walked up the front steps and opened the burgundy front door. "Mee-Maw," she called out. "We're here."

Mee-Maw didn't respond.

Ellie looked down at Louie. He lifted one of his large, heavy ears and listened. With a shake of his head, Ellie knew the house was empty.

"Must be at Uncle Jacob's." Ellie shrugged.

The cottage was one story with a bedroom and bathroom built off a modest living room-kitchen combination. The house was mostly clean, except for letters sprawled out on the table, along with a carafe of coffee and a half-empty mug.

Mee-Maw's friends. Ellie ignored the letters. *They're so weird.*

Other than her letters, Mee-Maw had nothing—no television, no internet—except she had an old radio that Ellie's father had to constantly repair. *She's a relic.*

"Guess Aunt Selena hasn't been by yet to clean," Ellie commented as she and Louie walked toward the backdoor.

Louie made it there first, and he sat, waiting for Ellie.

"You can stretch and wiggle but can't open doors?" Ellie teased him.

"No thumbs," he replied with a soft whine.

"Awww. Don't make the noise," Ellie said.

He whined again.

He's so adorable. Ellie set the water jug on the counter by the door, picked up Louie, and pulled him into a tight hug. "You're so fricken cute." She cooed and smothered him with kisses. Finally, Ellie put him down and opened the back door.

"I'll get a basket." Louie ran into the garden, out of sight.

"Get two," Ellie called out as she retrieved the water jug, which was covered in condensation. "Ah, crap," Ellie said, seeing that an envelope had stuck to her water jug. With careful fingers, she peeled the paper free.

Ellie wiped the wet envelope on her leg and double-checked the handwriting on the front of it to make sure it wasn't smeared.

Kevin Armitage

214 Seer St.

Oren, Maine 04283

Ellie pulled her head back questionably. *Kevin Armitage... why does that sound familiar?* She set the envelope back down on the counter and turned to the back door.

The rest of the farming continued seamlessly. Louie and Ellie munched on berries while they filled the crates, but neither Mee-Maw nor her mother showed up to help.

"I thought Mom was supposed to help, but I'm glad it was just you and me. I count that as a win," she told Louie as they walked back toward their house.

After lunch, Kimberly retreated to her library, which meant Louie and Ellie were free from additional chores.

"Do you want to build a tree fort?" Louie asked as his short legs hurried to keep up with Ellie's regular strides through the forest.

"No," Ellie muttered as they passed their sixth previous attempt at a tree fort.

"Catch bullfrogs at the pond?"

"Only you like that," she reminded him as she ducked beneath a low-hanging tree branch. *I could walk this path with my eyes closed.*

"They're so bouncy." Louie chuckled.

Even though she didn't want to go frog catching, she led them down the path, past the orchard, over the road, and out to the small pond by the river. The water was still, and the trees hung threateningly over the edge.

"Guess that happened from the winds during the last thunderstorm," Louie noted.

Ellie nodded. "It was a big one."

Ellie remembered that night. When the thunder first rumbled off in the distance, she and Louie ran outside so she could feel the static as it built in the air. The memory of it sent a chill down her spine.

Even though she could only manage short, quick connections with electricity, something about storms called to her.

Louie's laughter interrupted Ellie's memories. The hound sat back on his haunches and pointed into the reeds with a paw. "It looks so stupid!"

With a growing smile, Ellie walked to his side to see that Louie had singled out a fat, wart-covered frog. It stared back at Louie, unimpressed by the antics of the magical dog.

"How does it even..." He was laughing so hard, he couldn't finish his sentence. "Function?"

Having had enough of Louie's mockery, the frog hopped away, so Ellie and Louie sauntered around the pond, following the well-worn path the family had created over the years.

"It's Thursday," Ellie eventually announced on their third lap.

"We will get through tomorrow like we always do," Louie reassured her.

Friday carried the promise of two things: lasagna and a visit from Mee-Maw. Louie and Ellie would have to endure her judgmental looks, her snarky remarks, and her derogatory quips towards Louie.

"I just can't stand the way she talks to you," Ellie vented. "I think she's worse than Mom. If she brings up how you are meant to 'serve' me again, I'm gonna shock that old lady into a heart attack."

"What is it your dad always says... 'Don't judge a fly by its fish?'"
Louie hopped over the large rock on his side of the path.

Ellie snorted. "Don't judge a fish by its ability to fly?"

"Yes, that's the one... maybe she is only capable of seeing me in that
way. She can't think beyond that."

Ellie shoved her hands into her pocket as they walked. "Are you
saying you don't think Mee-Maw is capable of change?"

Louie walked with his thoughts for a minute. "I find humans remarkable. Some can do amazing things like hold their breath for...
how long was it?"

Ellie called back the documentary they watched months ago.
"Twenty minutes?"

"Yes, but look at you, in comparison, for example. You can't hold
yours for more than thirty seconds."

Ellie glared at him.

"It's like this. A flame is a flame, but if you feed the flame, it can be
a bomb fire, but with humans, even if you give them the right food, it
doesn't matter. They may end up being a genius, an Olympic athlete,
or like you..."

"Watch it," she warned.

"I'm not trying to be mean, just observant," Louie explained.
"You're normal."

"I'm a witch," she corrected him.

"You know what I'm saying." Louie rolled his eyes.

"Yeah. You're saying I'm a lazy dummy who can't hold her breath to
save her life." She kicked a pinecone.

"No. I'm saying that humans are weird." Louie kicked a loose rock
into their path. "Look at this rock. For all you know, it will always be
a rock. It takes millions of years to change into something else, but for
the lifetime of a human, a rock doesn't change."

"Right." Ellie stopped to observe.

"But you, you were a baby." A wide paw pointed at her.

"Okay. And?"

"As a baby, you learned, you evolved. You grew teeth, hair, a personality... you're unique."

Ellie raised an eyebrow. "You just said I was normal."

"A rock is a rock." He smacked it off of the path. "It can't react to my smack. It can't have an opinion or change itself or alter the world around it. But humans, you can sit on the couch or run a marathon or play an instrument. You can create something new. A rock can't."

"So, you're saying our free will separates us from rocks? Or our ability to change?"

"Yes, to an extent." He continued walking. "Humans can have varying characteristics and turn out remarkably similar. They can also have similar characteristics, be exposed to like environments, and be vastly different. Rocks don't have that range. Humans have range."

Ellie let that point sit in the air for a moment. "I'm confused. Are you upset about the plight of rocks? Or are you amazed by humans?"

"I'm amazed by your Mee-Maw's inability to do what comes so naturally to humans."

Ellie's smile grew wide. *I love getting under his skin.* "So, where do you stand on the rocks issue?" she teased.

"Forget the rocks, Ellie." The basset hound swatted her leg.

While Louie ran off to find more frogs to harass. Ellie stopped and dug up an old, broken mussel shell.

It wasn't surprising that Louie thought differently than she did. In his own words, he was a Familiar—a shooting star who traveled across the cosmos and through the Void to find her. She loved hearing the story of how he met their Seer and how it guided him through the darkness to Ellie.

"So, when do I get to talk to the famous Seer you told me about?" Ellie called out to Louie. "It sounds terrifying."

"Someday, I promise," he replied.

"I read that they're... odd. Is that true?" she asked as she caught up to Louie, who was staring at a buzzing dragonfly.

"They're not necessarily odd. They just don't think like we do."

"Like *we* do? Yeah right. You think differently than me, so I can't imagine how a seer must think."

A determined orange frog hopped after the dragonfly, and Louie excitedly followed the little frog. "You really think you're going to eat that, man? It's three times your size."

After Louie had his fill of frogs, they ended their stroll along the southern edge of the neighbor's apple orchard. Short grass tickled the back of Ellie's arms as she lay there, admiring the lazy view of the sky, speckled with wispy clouds. Birds chirped in the forest behind them, and the sweet smell of the apple blossoms drifted along the breeze.

"I don't want to stay in Connecticut," Ellie confessed. "I was thinking, if we were to go anywhere, we could go somewhere big."

"Big?" Louie lay on his back beside Ellie.

"Like big-big! Maybe Vegas big or like New Orleans big."

"That *is* big," Louie concurred.

Bzzzz. A fat bumble bee calmly drifted through the air and landed gracefully on top of a large flower with three bright-white petals. Louie leaped over Ellie, his paws barely missing the top of her stomach as he closed in on the bee.

"Buzz off!" Louie captured the bumblebee with a snap of his jaws. He quickly executed his prisoner with a concentrated flame from inside his mouth. Pleased by his excellent performance, he returned to Ellie's side.

"You spaz."

"It was coming right at you!" With a couple of indecisive circles, Louie lay back down at her side.

"It certainly was not." Ellie knew how stubborn Louie could be. Whenever it came to her safety, Louie made a fuss. Ellie affectionately petted his head. "Anyway, would you come with me? If I left Connecticut?"

"Of course. I'll never leave your side." With a yawn, Louie closed his eyes and leaned into Ellie's hand.

Thank the Void. Ellie felt the tightened muscles of her upper back ease. *Guess I just needed to hear him say it.*

The plan to leave Connecticut was all in her head and ever-changing. She wanted to see the rocky, unforgiving coast of Maine, the palm trees and everglades of Florida, the skyline of Boston, and Yellowstone with the geysers and bison. She also thought about New York and its buildings stretching to the sky.

Maybe we can go to a carnival. In movies, she had seen theme parks with wild pink candy that looked like clouds and guys who won girls massive teddy bears. *Make some friends... meet a guy.*

In her hazy thoughts, she drifted off to sleep and dreamed of a young man with carefully manicured facial hair passing her a large teddy bear and timidly sneaking a kiss—her first kiss.

3

Ouroboros

Hours had passed when a wet nose nudged her cheek. "Ellie, your dad whistled."

Ellie fought through the cloud of fogginess as Louie pulled her from her dream. A wet tongue licked her cheek, forcing her awake.

"Get up," Louie demanded. "We have to go back."

With him guiding the way, they walked the grueling distance back through the woods on the well-worn path toward their house.

"Ellie," Elijah called out. Before he could whistle a second time, Louie let out a gruff howl and rushed from the trees to meet Elijah, who kneeled in the doorway. Louie respectfully sat down in front of Elijah and accepted the gentle ear rubs. "There you two are. No issues?"

"Louie ate an innocent bee," Ellie reported, emphasizing her disapproval.

"He's just looking out for you, Sweetie." Elijah stepped aside and let the two enter.

Inside, the smell of something meaty, fatty, salty, and garlicky filled the air. Kimberly had made pot roast and fresh bread. Louie's nails clicked on the floor as the smell lured him to the dining room.

Three large white porcelain bowls were placed on top of decorative plates on the circular table in the large dining room. Each place setting had a matching side dish adorned with beautiful roses and golden leaves. A red plastic bowl sat on the floor by Ellie's side.

"Every time," Ellie grumbled loudly.

She took the belittling bowl and placed it at her side on the wooden table. Then, she pulled a chair around as Louie dragged a large pillow into the room.

Good. He got the booster pillow.

In a well-practiced and coordinated effort, Louie donned the chair with the booster pillow; then, Ellie placed Louie on his throne beside her.

Elijah entered the room carrying a deep white stone dish. He set it in the center of the table. Unpeeled red potatoes, full baby carrots, and onions were neatly placed on one side of the dish, garnished with bits of fresh rosemary and parsley. The other side of the dish had large chunks of fresh, saucy beef.

"Dog! Get the wine," Kimberly barked from the kitchen.

"Don't order him around like that," Ellie snapped.

"It's okay." Louie hopped down and disappeared from the dining room toward the pantry across from the kitchen. Then, Louie returned to the dining room with an unopened bottle of wine in his mouth.

Elijah gently took it from him. "Hm, what'd you get for us tonight?" he mused and looked over the label. "A merlot? Good choice." Elijah gave Louie an approving pat on the head.

Louie returned to his throne beside Ellie, and Kimberly emerged from the kitchen with a woven basket lined with a gingham cloth. Ellie watched as her mother gawked at the red bowl, and then Kimberly glared at Louie. She let out a disgusted sigh through her tight, slender nose.

Ellie glared back at her. *I dare you to say something.*

Kimberly sucked air between her teeth before she turned to the table and put the basket of bread down.

Good.

With everyone seated, Elijah poured wine for Kimberly and himself. Then, he fixed Kimberly's plate for her. Ellie patiently waited. It was a family rule for the cook to be served first as a sign of gratitude.

"Thank you, darling," Kimberly said.

"All the thanks to you." Elijah nodded at Ellie to let her know she could make her plate.

Much to Kimberly's disapproval, Ellie served Louie first.

"Bread?" Elijah asked and held out a large slice for Louie.

Louie gently accepted it in his teeth and placed it on the edge of the bowl.

He tries so hard, Ellie thought as Louie nudged the bread into the perfect spot so it wouldn't fall.

"Anything fun happen at work today?" Ellie asked, looking at her father.

"As you know, nothing 'fun' happens in accounting, and if something out of the ordinary *did* happen, then it'd be someone else's concern. How about you two?"

Louie said he'd come with me if I left Connecticut. She shook that thought away. "Besides the close encounter with the bee?"

"Oh yeah, that's right." Elijah held up his index finger as he chewed. "A feat of such bravery certainly earns a second slice of bread." Elijah placed a fat heel piece in Louie's bowl.

"Did you have your EpiPen?" Kimberly asked.

"No need when I have the Bee Bully here." Ellie gently touched Louie's back.

"You should really keep that on you, honey. You don't want to risk—"

"It's just hives, Mom," Ellie spat out.

"Which could eventually turn into anaphylaxis. You need that pen in case that ever happens."

"You're right." Ellie knew this was the only way to put this subject to rest. "I'll remember next time I leave the house."

"Thank you." Kimberly grabbed Elijah's hand. He gave her a gentle squeeze.

For a few minutes, everything was silent except the sounds of forks scraping against bowls and the clinks of wine glasses.

"My dear, how was your day? Any new discoveries?" Elijah asked his wife, breaking the silence.

Ellie smirked. Her mother had tons of theories, but Ellie's favorite was the discovery that a zoonotic virus killed the North American Sasquatch off like the plague, swine flu, or even HIV.

"No new discoveries, per se, but you know the ouroboros?" Kimberly asked as she lifted her wine glasses.

"That's the um, the..." As Elijah searched for the word, he drew a circle in the air with his fork.

"Serpent," Louie provided.

"Yes!" Elijah pointed a fork of approval in Louie's direction. "Thank you. The snake that eats its own tail."

"Correct." Kimberly nodded toward Elijah, ignoring Louie. "Well, it's mentioned in the tomb of Tutankhamun, dated in the fourteenth century BCE, fifth century BCE in China, and again in third century Alexandria. It's also reflected in Scandinavia as Jörmungandr, a sea serpent who wraps around the world and bites its tail at the other end."

Kimberly's words hung in the air like she expected Elijah to finish her thought.

Oh, just say it already. The silence was killing her, so Ellie chimed in. "Maybe each culture happened to see an overheated, confused snake eat its own tail."

Kimberly's bright eyes turned toward Ellie. Intrigued, she waved her hand for Ellie to continue.

"We—" She gestured to Louie. "Saw it on television. When snakes in captivity get stressed, hungry, or overheated, they get confused and start to eat their own tails. You gotta cool it down, or it'll die because it digests itself."

"So, you're suggesting this recurring mythological creature is actually the result of a natural phenomenon?" her mother challenged.

"Absolutely. This isn't like Big Foot or Wendigos or something. We could probably walk into a crappy Pets & Stuff and see it. People who were studying the world back then, scientists, priests, and such, probably had lots of pets and didn't take care of them. Like that guy with the cat in the box?"

"Schrödinger?" Kimberly raised an eyebrow.

"Yeah! That guy who tortured cats," Ellie said.

"He wasn't—" Kimberly tried to correct the misunderstanding, but Ellie ran over her like a steamroller.

"They're all sadists. They probably observed it and thought it was an act of 'the Gods' or something and documented it." Ellie mumbled quickly to Louie, "Something crazy like how they thought the world was flat." She took a bite of bread.

Kimberly looked pensive. "That's a good hypothesis."

Elijah beamed with pride as his eyes glanced between his wife and daughter.

"Now," Ellie continued. "Sea serpents, water serpents—those are seen across cultures, right, Mom? China, Japan, North America. They all talk about massive water snakes—not like our little local guys." Ellie demonstrated their size with her hands. "They're talking about anaconda-sized snakes in chilly places where they can't survive. I could get behind that being magical."

"Why wouldn't they be able to survive in cold environments?" Kimberly had stabbed her fork into a large piece of meat in her bowl but had little interest in eating it. She leaned forward.

"They're cold-blooded and need the sun to keep their bodies warm."

"Are you implying that snakes don't live in colder environments?" Kimberly pressed.

"Well, of course not. We have garter snakes and Northern Water Snakes, but they go underground to hibernate."

"Brumate," Louie corrected her.

"Thank you. Yes, brumate," Ellie said with a smile.

"So why can't we have an anaconda?" Kimberly pushed.

Ellie was stumped. She looked to Louie for help, but Elijah butted in quickly. "No help from the peanut gallery. This is your point; finish it."

"It's too cold?" Ellie paused.

"Think about it this way." Kimberly sat back in her chair, abandoning her skewered meat. "It takes a lot of energy to heat your room. We could use a space heater for that. We *couldn't* use a space heater to warm this house, though, right? It takes a lot more energy, a greater source, to power something so large. Now, consider the sun as one big power source. You take into account the directness or length of exposure of the sun to the land, the animals on it. With the Earth tilted at an angle, certain areas have more direct and closer exposure to the heat source. *That* is what allows us to have winter—and why they wouldn't have snow and winter in the Amazon. That's why they have different animal life, different plant life. A bigger object needs a larger, more direct power source. Anaconda-sized water snakes wouldn't get the heat they need to survive in Connecticut."

"So, I wasn't wrong," Ellie said.

"You weren't wrong, but you weren't at your conclusion," Kimberly pointed out. "You needed to do more digging to get there."

Of course, nothing is good enough. Ellie shook her head gently from side to side. She stabbed a potato on her plate. When she looked up, she saw an exchange between her parents. Her father stared with adoring eyes at her mother, who blushed. With a shaking breath, Kimberly fanned herself.

Aren't they cute?

"Well done, Ellie," Elijah praised his daughter.

After dinner, Ellie and Louie cleaned. Louie licked the plates clean, and Ellie loaded them into the dishwasher. Kimberly had retreated to the library, but Elijah arranged a plate of chocolates and poured her a glass of red wine.

As he passed Ellie and Louie on the way to the library, he said, "It's the little things that keep the magic alive."

"I hope I have a marriage like theirs one day," Ellie muttered as she finished washing the dishes that wouldn't fit inside the dishwasher.

"I am sure you will."

After they cleaned the kitchen, Ellie and Louie cuddled up on her bed and watched reruns of a late '80s family-friendly sitcom on her small boxy television, but Ellie couldn't focus on the show. She looked over the wrinkled brochure for the University of Massachusetts in Boston. She had opened and closed it so many times that the creases were worn and torn. With an irritated sigh, she shoved the brochure back into her nightstand. Then, she lay back flat on the bed, and Louie put his head on her shoulder.

"Thinking about Boston?" Louie asked as she ran her fingers over the top of his head.

"Boston, New Orleans, New York..."

"Yellow Stone," Louie added.

Ellie smirked and let out a long sigh. "I hear they can't see the night sky like this in New York. Too many lights from the city."

4

Leverage and Dragons

With each thrust of its mighty wings, the dragon brought *Princess Nina closer to the ragged mountain's peak.*

"Hang on, Sloan," she whispered as she drew her sword. "I'll save you. I promise."

"Kimberly!" Mother shrieked, pulling fourteen-year-old Kimberly from her book.

Kimberly sat timidly behind a barricade of cleaning supplies in the back of the closet. *Crap!*

Jean, one of Kimberly's older sisters, had given their mother the nickname, 'The Dastardly Dragon of the Backcountry.' Kimberly thought it fit—especially now, since her mother was banging on the closet door. The handle jiggled. Thank goodness it had a tendency to stick.

Kimberly hid her precious book behind the mop bucket. *The dragon'll never look there.*

The door handle jiggled again. "What are you doing in there?"

"I got stuck grabbing the... uh..." She couldn't say mop bucket. "The... this!" Panicked, she grabbed the duster.

Just then, the door swung open, and Mother's swollen, pregnant belly inched into the frame of the doorway. "You dusted yesterday," she hissed through clenched teeth.

Think quickly, think quickly. Kimberly swallowed hard. "I found a cobweb in Jean's... in... uh... in my closet."

Ever since her older sister Jean ran away, the shared bedroom belonged only to Kimberly. Even though Mother got rid of every scrap of Jean's existence, she couldn't remove the window she snuck out of, the closet her clothes once populated, or the sweater Kimberly stole back time and time again.

"Are you saying you did a sloppy..." Mother interrupted herself with a gasp.

Oh no, oh no.

"What..." Mother paused between words and enunciated, "are you wearing?"

Crap! Kimberly froze.

"You went through the trash again, didn't you? I told you! I don't want any of that ungrateful brat's things in this house!" Like an untamed beast, Mother clawed through the cleaning supplies and threw anything in her path out into the hallway. Bottles broke, liquids flowed, and feathers decorated the air. Mother grabbed the invaluable sweater, tearing it from Kimberly's frame. "Take it off!"

Kimberly struggled against the wall Mother pinned her to. Desperately, she cried out, "Careful, Mom! Careful, or you could hurt the baby."

"I'll worry about the baby! That's my job."

With shaking knees, Kimberly buckled to the floor as the final scraps of Jean were torn away.

"We all have our duties," Mother hissed, but her voice faltered. "You don't get to j-just choose not to follow through!"

Kimberly looked away. She knew Mother was talking about Jean and how she ran away before she could get married to the Canadian boy, Simon Gagnon.

"Your father may have taken the lazy way out, and that little brat may have dodged her duties, but I saw to it that Kelly fulfilled her duties, knocked up or not, and *you* will fulfill your duties too!"

"Yes, Mother," Kimberly squeaked.

"You will *not* be my greatest failure, Kimberly. Do you understand me?" Mother shouted.

Kimberly once again became too aware of her mark-less scalp. Mother loved to remind her of her greatest shortcoming—the one she couldn't do anything about. Without a gift from the Void, she couldn't make potions.

"Yes, Mother." Kimberly's voice dropped.

"We all have a job to do," Mother spat. "What's your job?"

"T-t-to take care of—"

"Wrong!" Mother smacked the wall with the wooden spoon in her hand.

"To marry and have babies with marks," Kimberly added quickly.

"That's right." Mother pointed her wooden spoon directly at the plump little girl curled up on the floor. "You will marry *who* I say, *when* I say."

"Yes, ma'am." Kimberly didn't dare look up. Her bottom lip trembled. It had been years since Jean was there to step in between them, to protect her from Mother's spoon, to share the load. *Why did you leave me here?*

As Mother stomped out of the closet, something clattered, and she grumbled to herself down the hallway. When Kimberly finally emerged, she saw the potentially toxic puddle on the floor and sponges strewn out like confetti. The metal dustpan sat upside down at the other end of the hallway just before the kitchen door, where Mother stood with the sweater in hand.

"There's only one way to ensure I never see this hideous sweater again."

Kimberly knew the sound of the cast-iron stove's lid as it scraped loudly.

"No." She gasped and ran off down the hallway with no concern for her bare feet through the mess. Even though her left foot caught on the dustpan and gashed the side of it open, she kept moving. Kimberly came around the corner just in time to see the flames lick up the last bit of wool in the edge of the metal tongs.

"Jean," Kimberly shrieked.

***

Friday-Present Day

Kimberly's glasses sat low on the bridge of her nose as she reread the tale of the Jörmungandr.

Banished into the sea by Oden, Jörmungandr was able to grow to such an incredible size that the beast could circle the globe. It held its own tail in its mouth...

Or each culture happened to see an overheated, confused snake eat its own tail. Ellie's words about improper snake care tormented her. Kimberly sucked air between her teeth.

"Ugh, weeks of reading and researching down the drain," she complained to herself. "It's so simple... I must be losing my touch."

She shut the text and wrote in her personal journal: Natural Phenomenon.

Still need to double-check that information, though... have Elijah pick up a manual on snake care when he's in town. Kimberly yawned, pulled off her glasses, and rubbed her tired eyes. "Either way, a job well done."

She stood from her plush armchair and shuffled across the hardwood floor in her cozy slippers. A smile crept across her face as Kimberly admired her double-layered bookshelf. As a token of his adoration, Elijah designed and built it for her to house all her journals, books, and sources in the small den. She slid her book, *Tales from the Depths—Scandinavian Folklore*, onto one of the shelves.

"Perfect. Everything is in its place."

Years of Kimberly's hard work and dedication sat on display before her. Each book was carefully labeled with her own form of the Dewey Decimal System.

This is my job, she told herself. *To restore our history and educate my girl.*

Kimberly looked around in the library, and she smiled. In this room, she didn't have to hide her tears, her frustrations, or her worries. The library was hers alone—the refurbished office space Elijah dedicated to her the first day she moved in with her husband twenty-seven years earlier.

Kimberly sat down in the wide olive-green armchair and looked down at the handmade rug filled with strips of different cotton shirts under the chair. It was a birthday present from Ellie many years ago—before puberty and that dog.

Don't think about that stupid dog, she told herself. She glanced up at the hand-painted family tree on the wall in front of her. Seeing her husband's name, she smiled, stood, and walked over to the expansive artwork. Tenderly, she brushed her fingers over the delicate, thoughtfully designed cursive lettering.

Above his name, along the line that connected them, was her darling daughter's name—Ellie-Lynne Betty Becker. Kimberly frowned, seeing the small star next to her Ellie's name, which indicated she had a Familiar.

That useless little leech. Kimberly's nostrils flared with anger. *He's supposed to serve her, protect her. To be her soldier!*

Betty Fischer's prophecy lingered in Kimberly's mind.

That dog's dead weight. An actual basset hound would have been a better addition to the family.

"Awooo!" Howling cut off her thoughts, and Kimberly snapped to attention.

"Oh no!" She whipped open the old wooden door of her library and rushed toward the front porch. Louie stood in the gravel driveway lined with bright pink azalea bushes. He bared his teeth at a vile, unwanted creature: a salesman.

"Louie!" Kimberly clapped her hands. "Come back."

Obediently, Louie backed up toward the porch.

When Ellie emerged around the corner, Kimberly noticed her dirty arms and a streak of soil across her cheek. She brandished a trowel in her gloved hands, her hair tied back by an old red bandana. Breathless, she asked, "What happened?"

"It's nothing, honey. Take the dog out back," Kimberly replied.

"Come on, Louie." He followed Ellie, and with one last glance, the duo turned around the corner.

"At least he's good for something," Kimberly muttered to herself.

"Quite the guard dog you have there," the salesman joked.

Kimberly's eyes narrowed as she took him in. *Jeans and a T-shirt? What happened to the days when door-to-door vacuum salesmen wore suits? No pride.*

She crossed her arms over her chest. "You didn't come all this way to talk about the dog. Cut to the chase."

The young man awkwardly chuckled and shifted his clipboard between his hands. "Starting to feel like maybe I was better off with the dog." He fanned himself with the collar of his t-shirt before he dove into his sales pitch. "Well, ma'am, I'm with Diamond Fiber Optics. We're now offering fiber optic internet services throughout-"

"No thanks!" She knew what this was. Kimberly may have lived in the countryside, but she wasn't born yesterday. Elijah had to use it at work, and it could stay there, as far as she was concerned. All the information she needed to teach her child, to do her research, could come from books.

"It's a great service," he added with desperation in his voice. "Great upload speeds, uh, for streaming movies, music, videos."

Kimberly's nostrils flared. Her foot tapped gently against the wooden porch.

"Um, your daughter could take college classes online and message her..."

Online classes, college classes. That's it! I can keep her safe at home from that prophecy. We can buy time on the marriage proposals, and we won't risk violating anything. Mother may even be on board.

"I'm so sorry. Where are my manners?" Kimberly donned a polite, helpful customer-service smile and hurried off the porch. "My husband is at work; do you have any literature about your services? A business card, perhaps?"

5

Pain Relief

Beads of sweat rolled down Ellie's brow and dripped off the tip of her nose as she covered another small vegetable plant with dirt.

"Stake." Ellie put out her hand like a surgeon awaiting an instrument.

"Sh-tayk." Louie firmly placed a birch branch into her palm.

"Twine."

With the help of her skilled assistant, the operation was a success, with the small, budding plant properly secured. Plants lined the mound that stretched all the way back to the other end of the fence line.

"I need a break." Ellie sat back on the walking path. Before her, another ten feet of empty ground was ready for small vegetable plants, and all of them would need staking, too.

"I'll get you some lemonade," Louie said happily and scuttled off towards the house.

"Thank you," she called. "You're my favorite!"

"I know," he yelled. "But you can always remind me."

The back door creaked as he opened it.

"This is going to take forever," Ellie complained to the sky above. She would need more than lemonade to feel refreshed after all this.

She wiped at her forehead with the back of her forearm, leaving a smear of dirt on her face.

Gross.

Fridays were always like this—stressful, messy, and nerve-wracking. They had so much to do before Mee-Maw's visit, and Ellie's nervous-nelly mom would see that everything was perfect.

Since Mother's Day had passed, the threat of frost was behind them in New England, so Ellie worked between the two gardens every day to get the pre-started plants in the ground. Aside from Mee-Maw's bullish reputation for being a strict disciplinarian, she was also known for her remarkable power: the ability to help plants grow.

According to Ellie's mother, Mee-Maw's power had suitors lined up at the door when she was a young woman. Ellie hadn't even had one suitor yet.

Thank the Void.

As common as arranged marriages were, Ellie had bigger dreams for romance. She wanted a boy to swoon her like they did in the movies on television. She wanted the thrilling experience of dating and maybe even cuddling with a crush under a starry sky. Though she didn't want any suitors, she still wondered why none of the boys had tried.

Am I ugly? She caught herself asking that time and time again. *Is my gift that pathetic?*

Ellie thought about the time Mee-Maw drunkenly complained about Ellie's power. "Is that it?" she had shrieked.

Sitting beside Mee-Maw, Ellie looked to her mother, expecting her to say something, but of course, Kimberly froze.

"It's because of your father," Mee-Maw continued, addressing Kimberly. "You know, his sister didn't have any powers. Marrying him was an act of charity. I coulda' been paired with Conrad Hurst, you know? I woulda' been right on the council, his right-hand, and everyone would know it! But no. My mother didn't look out for me like I looked out for you. She saddled me up with that dead horse, and here we are. We had to make a deal with that Becker, which landed us in the middle-of-no-where Connecticut. You with no powers, and her with pathetic little..."

Just then, the bottle of half-empty wine fell to its side, and burgundy liquid spilled onto the table and dripped onto the wooden floor.

"Oh! My tablecloth," Kimberly fussed.

Ellie looked over at Louie, who had donned an innocent expression, but he shot Ellie a quick wink.

"The wine," Mee-Maw cried.

Ellie never wanted to go through an experience like that again, but her father would be home tonight, so Mee-Maw probably wouldn't go off on a rant. Ellie couldn't understand it, but Mee-Maw seemed less inclined to act up around Elijah.

The backdoor creaked open once again, and Louie padded toward her, carrying a hand-woven basket in his mouth containing a mason jar filled with fresh lemonade.

"Thank you, sir." She sat up and took the glass jar in her hand. "Violets? Nice touch."

"Now, take a break. I will start the holes." Louie trotted down the path and dug holes for the small plants. "Do I need to add holes for Skunk Butts?"

"Not yet," she called back. Skunk Butts was the nickname she gave to marigolds after she first sniffed them as a child. Ellie took a gulp of her lemonade. "We need to wait for the old woman to grow some."

"She seems to be getting weaker in her years," Louie called back as his two front paws aggressively dug into the dirt. "Oh, a grub!" With an excited pounce, he squashed it. "Not today, mister bug."

A smirk crossed Ellie's lips as she watched him work. He never seemed to grow tired like she did.

When he finished his line of holes, Louie returned to Ellie and laid his big head on her thigh. "I can't handle the plants, or I will break them."

Ellie set the remainder of the icy lemonade beside him. "Your turn for a break."

The morning turned into the afternoon by the time the two had the garden in an acceptable condition for Mee-Maw's visit. Exhausted and in desperate need of a shower, Ellie meandered inside with Louie trailing behind her.

After they finished lunch, Ellie turned to Louie and said, "Oh, we still have to make the wench's pain relief remedy." She groaned loudly.

"I heard that," Kimberly called from down the hallway. Ellie glared in her general direction, then stuck her tongue out.

Louie chuckled and hopped off his chair. "Too tired to make the potion-lotion?"

"Yeah, I'm drained. The sun took it out of me."

"I'd be happy to help you if you need a little boost," he offered.

Ellie raised an eyebrow at the basset hound. "You?"

"Yeah, I *am* from the Void, after all," he reminded her. "Gimme a chance."

Louie had never helped Ellie infuse a potion or a potion-lotion before. Now, he sat back on his haunches and donned sad, pleading eyes while he whimpered softly.

"So not fair." Ellie sighed. "Fine," she said as she gathered the ingredients.

***

Ellie checked that she had everything—a wide-mouthed sixteen-ounce glass jar, a metal scoop for carving ceramics, and an emulsifier.

"That's a big jar," Louie commented.

"Gonna make a double batch." Ellie wiggled her eyebrows with a mischievous grin.

"You think she'll use all of that in a week?"

"No," she admitted and began to prepare her ingredients. "But maybe, if she has enough for two weeks, she won't come by next week."

She split open a fresh aloe leaf and scraped the gel into the glass jar.

"She could make the potion herself if she didn't want to come by," Louie reminded her. "She just wants to drink wine and make everybody miserable."

Ellie's shoulders sank. She hated to admit it, but he was probably right. "Well, we will see."

She carefully peeled ginger and ground up dried willow bark. The moment the bark hit the aloe gel, it leeched a hideous yellow coloration into it. With the rest of the ingredients roughly stirred into the concoction, Ellie shoved in the emulsifier and allowed it to work its mechanical magic. After a minute, the crude amalgamation sat ready for her to infuse.

Ellie drew a large circle in chalk on top of the workbench and turned off the lights. "Alright, time for the fun part," she said.

Louie hopped into Ellie's lap and set his paws on top of the workstation.

As simple as "channeling the Void" sounded, it could be demanding on the body, especially if someone wasn't used to doing it every day. Ellie was already exhausted from their chores, so she was glad Louie was helping her today.

"Are you ready?" she asked him.

"I was born ready!" Louie shifted his weight in her lap from side to side. She called this his "Happy Paws Dance."

"Okay, calm down. We have to focus." Ellie grabbed his unsettled paws and guided them up to the edge of the symbol.

Ellie counted down, "Three... two... one..."

In unison, they took a deep breath, then slowly exhaled. This wasn't a part of the actual ritual but more a part of Ellie's personal ritual to help her center herself and focus, much like she did for her morning meditations. After a few rounds of concentrated, focused breaths, they were ready.

With a bow of her head, Ellie hummed softly. She didn't hum a familiar tune or anything fancy, just a simple, low note Louie could connect with. And he did.

Once their hums were in harmony, the mark on top of Ellie's head grew warm. Much to her surprise, the furry bundle in her lap also grew warm. Sparkles and twinkles of light beyond her closed eyelids let her know they were within the peripherals of the Void.

A splendid, familiar tickle ran down her spine, through her core, and out through her extremities. The Void connected and affected everybody a bit differently. Some found it uncomfortable and avoided it at all costs, but for Ellie, it was odd and delightful.

Today, the Void felt different, though. It felt more pleasant than the soft tickle she was accustomed to feeling. For a moment, she greedily leaned into the sensation, but a sharp claw dug into her hand, pulling her back into focus. The interruption took her concentration from her breath and tore her from harmonization with Louie, which should have closed off her connection.

"Push it out," she heard Louie say, but it wasn't quite his voice. No, he was still humming. It was like a part of him, something otherworldly, speaking to her—or speaking *around* her.

Push what out? she thought, and it was as if her voice echoed through her own mind.

"Don't let it draw you in," a feminine voice reverberated through the air around her.

"Who's that?" Ellie called out. "Who's there?"

"It's okay." Louie's presence overcame her like a warm embrace. "It's your Seer. She's guiding us."

"The Void gives, and the Void takes," her voice came back.

"A creature of darkness..."

"Save them, Ellie..."

"To become one..."

"A soulmate..."

The voices overlapped, and she couldn't tell who was saying what. It was as if she was the center point of disjointed thoughts, all fighting for her attention. Ellie felt her own breath shake, and the pleasant warmth in her hands started to burn.

"Silence," Louie demanded in a tone Ellie had never heard him use before. "She needs to focus."

And in that moment, all was still, but the burning in Ellie's hands remained. "It hurts."

"Stop holding on to it. Push the Void's essence *through* your hands, Ellie," Louie and the reverberating voice simultaneously instructed.

Ellie concentrated on pushing her breath through her vocal cords to be in harmony with Louie, but sustaining the hum felt like she was trying to talk through a terrible cold. With a crack, she reached the same note once again, and the connection was the catalyst she needed to set off a series of explosions. The Void, the warmth, and the orange glow all rushed forward into her hands like a crack of lightning. It was incredible!

BAM!

The force knocked Ellie and Louie from the stool back onto the wooden floor of the pantry. Behind Ellie's head, Louie somehow broke her fall.

"You okay?" It was weird to hear his voice sound normal now. She reached back and touched him. He felt fuzzy. With a sigh of relief, she dropped her hands to the floor.

"Yeah... yeah. You?"

"Yeah. It was weird being back..." His voice trailed off. "Oh, look!"

Before them, on the workbench, the symbol had stopped glowing. The only glow in the room now came from the kitchen and the jar of potion-lotion that wobbled from side to side, slowing from an intense spin.

"Wow!" Ellie exclaimed. "It's never done this before."

The glow from the jar was like a beacon in the night. Normally, it could barely be compared to the glow of an oil lamp.

"Told you I was powerful," Louie said.

"This is not the time for an 'I told you so.'"

Slowly, the light faded, and the jar became stable. Ellie climbed to her feet and inspected the jar. It looked completely normal.

"Is it safe to give to her?" Ellie asked as she set it back down.

"It should be. Are you sure you're okay?" Louie tried to pull the stool back upright. The screech of wood against wood pulled Ellie's attention to him.

"Yeah, I just... yeah." Ellie looked down at her hands. The gentlest tingle remained, and her skin was blotchy.

"Let me see your hands," Louie demanded.

"I told you they're fine."

"No, you said you were fine, which I don't believe." He inspected her hands. "You can't hold on to the essence like that. You need to let it flow through you."

"I can't stop it if I don't know I'm doing it," she countered.

"When you feel that heat build in your hands?"

"Yeah."

"Push it out." He let go of her hand.

"What will happen if I don't?"

"Besides getting burned?" Louie shook his head. "You know that tingle? That sensation you were being pulled towards?"

Ellie flinched away from him. "I wasn't..." Then she remembered when his claw dug into her and pulled her back into focus. "Yeah... I remember."

"It draws you in by giving you something to enjoy. The Void gives, and the Void takes," he said, repeating the Seer's words. He looked at Ellie expectantly, but she still looked confused. "The Void can take many things... including you, Ellie."

6

❦

Dinner

For the rest of the afternoon, they cleaned, per Ellie's mother's instructions. They scrubbed counters, washed windows, and mopped floors.

When they were finally on their last task, making tomato sauce for the night's lasagna, Ellie turned to Louie. "So, the Void is different for you?" she asked.

"Well, yes, I spent my life there," Louie explained. "But I'm not an organic being like you. You've never seen me bleed, right?"

"Well, yeah, but I just... I guess I just thought you were careful."

"Smells delicious," Kimberly mused as she came around the corner and donned her apron.

"Thanks." Ellie yawned and walked to the sink to wash the smell of onions and garlic from her hands. Mechanically, she applied soap and lathered her hands together as she looked out at the backyard. Rows and rows of happy, healthy plants stood at the far end. Ellie looked down as she rinsed off her hands, but the blotchy redness remained. *Do I need to put something on it?*

"Everything alright?" Kimberly asked as she walked to the cupboard beside Ellie. Ellie quickly pulled her hands away from the sink and wiped them on her pants.

"Yeah, I'm fine." Kimberly was the last person Ellie wanted to talk to about what happened with the potion-lotion. Well, that was a lie. *Mee-Maw* was the last person she wanted to talk to, but Kimberly was a close second.

"Excited to see Mee-Maw?" Kimberly seemed oddly chipper.

"No?" Ellie looked at her mother skeptically. "Why? Are you?"

"Come on, she hasn't been that bad in a while. Don't you think?" Kimberly replied.

"Yeah, and I'm sure Hitler was pleasant in the mornings."

"Ellie-Lynne!"

Ellie shrugged. "You asked."

On that note, Ellie scooped Louie in her arms and made a break for their room. There was only an hour left until her dad would be home.

I'll talk to Dad about it. Hopefully, he'll understand. Plus, he'd never bring it up to Mee-Maw, she reassured herself before she gently placed Louie amongst the plush pillows.

Ellie and Louie lay on the bed and stared at the off-white, stucco ceiling. Now, without a chore to distract her or her mother to pick a fight with, Ellie felt the effects of the hangover from drawing from the Void.

With a foggy brain, she mentally walked through the scenario for the hundredth time: the preparation, the doubling of the batch... Louie in her lap—every little thing. Her mind drifted as she remembered the warmth, the glow in the darkness, and the way Louie sounded—his ethereal embrace surrounding the Seer's voice.

Don't let it draw you in. The words rang through her mind. Somehow, it was distant, yet so present.

***

"Ellie," Kimberly's soft voice broke through her distant thoughts. She felt a hand gently wiggling her foot, which roused her out of her sleepiness.

"Mm, what?" Ellie lifted her head only to feel the weight of Louie's head on her chest. She could barely find the strength to push him off.

"Are you feeling okay?" her mom asked with a sweet smile and concerned eyes.

Ellie's head ached, and her mind lazily floated along like it was stuck in one of those theme-park rivers. "Yeah. What's up? What do you need?"

"You need to finish your lasagna and get dressed. Your grandma will be here soon."

Ugh. "Right."

Louie lifted his head off her chest, and Ellie sat up. She kissed the top of Louie's head and rubbed his back.

"I'll make you some coffee. You're going to need to brush your hair," Kimberly said before leaving.

That's the last thing I need, a Kimberly Becker fuss-fest, Ellie thought as she forced herself to follow her mother into the kitchen.

Tired and foggy, Ellie stood in front of the heavy ceramic stone dish on the countertop. Sauce, noodle layer, cheese. Sauce, noodle layer, cheese.

"Cream?" Kimberly placed a mug before Ellie. Steam danced from the brim of the bright orange ceramic mug.

"Please."

At knee level, Louie held up the red, heavy, deep stone lid for Ellie. It was so large, it blocked him from her view. Ellie took the lid from him with both hands, placed it on top of the dish, and put the lasagna into the hot oven.

Kimberly set the timer beside the stove. "Now, go get dressed. You know she'll have a cow if you're in pants," Kimberly instructed.

"I'm so not ready for this," Ellie groaned and dragged her feet back to her bedroom with Louie in tow. "Help me pick something out?"

"Violet! The violet one." Louie dove into the closet. Too short to reach the hangers, Louie stretched up, took the dress in his mouth, and harassed it off the hanger.

Louie apparently doesn't get the Void-hangover, she thought as she sipped her coffee and tried to do something with her hair. Fly aways and unruly curls bounced at the sides of her head. "Are you feeling alright?" Ellie asked Louie.

"I am happy." A familiar thump behind her indicated Louie had hopped off the bed. She anticipated his touch before she even felt the pressure of his paw on her outer left thigh.

"You're not tired or anything?" Ellie took some bobby pins from the top of her wooden desk and separated the taut metal with her bottom row of teeth.

"No, I napped," he said matter-of-factly and brought over a cream-colored hair clip for Ellie.

With his assistance, she settled for a half-up hairdo secured by the small clip and bobby pins. The rest of her curly, dark-mahogany hair bounced down past her shoulders. She still looked tired, but this would do.

"Perfect, now for the dress." Louie led her over to the bed. She swore if his tail were more propeller-shaped, he would fly with how fast it moved. Politely, he turned away as she got dressed. "You did amazing with that potion."

"I barely did anything." Ellie was careful not to mess up her hair as she slid the violet dress overhead. "I'm dressed. You can turn around," Ellie mumbled.

"You did a lot more than you know." He stared at her. "Gorgeous."

"I swear, if you were a boy, you'd make me blush." A lighthearted chuckle escaped her lips, and she adjusted her dress. "Is it tucked right?"

Louie responded with a floppy-eared nod.

She rubbed her tired face and reached for the cup of coffee. *I can't believe nobody has made a remedy for exhaustion.* She sat down on her bed, put her elbows on her knees, and took a sip. "Can you grab me the blue bow on the clip?" Ellie asked.

Happily, Louie obliged. When he returned to her with the accessory from her vanity, she took it from his lips and attached it to his collar.

"You're the most adorable thing I have ever seen," she said, with a kiss on his nose. As she pulled back from her fuzzy, brown-eyed friend, his earlier words floated through her mind. *I'm not an organic being like you.* "Bud?"

"Mm?"

"What you said earlier about living in the Void... you wouldn't be pulled apart like I would be?"

He nodded. "Correct."

"So, if I were stuck in the Void, I'd be destroyed, but you'd just sit there? Like, what did you do when you were in the Void—before you met me?" Ellie pictured the Void as an endless space of darkness.

"I found Seer, and I found your puddle." He tilted his head to the side. "It's not like I went sightseeing or held a job up there."

Ellie's eyebrows furrowed together with confusion. "So, you just sat there for fourteen years?"

Louie sat back thoughtfully. "Time doesn't work the same way there as it does here. It doesn't stand still, but... I don't know how to describe it. There are stars and the cosmos above you, but there is no way to tell time—no sundials, no clocks, no morning or night. For me, it didn't feel like fourteen years. I guess I didn't have much of a context or feel for time until I came to Earth."

Through the hall, the sound of the screen door echoed as it shut.

"Eli!" Kimberly was always happy and excited to see Elijah when he came home, but today she sounded extra excited.

"Weird," Ellie said. It wasn't strange that her mom was happy, but it was weird for her to be giddy on a Friday. "Why isn't she a neurotic mess?"

Louie shrugged.

"Well, keep an eye out," Ellie said as she sipped the remaining cooled bit of coffee. "She's up to something."

Louie responded with a fat-armed salute and waddled off to the bedroom door, where he stood watch. She got one more sip of her coffee before he told her, "They're going into the library."

"Oh really?" The library was a coveted space where research and discussions 'inappropriate for the ears of children' were conducted.

Ellie set her mug on the nightstand and tiptoed to the door where Louie stood. Together, they leaned out and listened.

Silence.

Ellie looked down at Louie, and he stared back up at her. She nodded, and the duo covertly made their way down the hallway to an old brass vent behind the large armchair in the living room. They curled there and placed their ears against the vent.

"Kimberly, we can't accept any of these," Elijah pleaded. "She's only met them all, maybe once. How can we ask her to marry a complete stranger?"

Ellie stiffened as she listened. *Marry?*

"*You* were a complete stranger," Kimberly countered.

"It's completely different. We were both on board with this decision, and we were a part of the process—not like this. We're only two years apart. Not... what is it..." Ellie heard papers shuffle. "Armitage is fifteen years older than her. Cambro is seventeen. The only mildly acceptable option is Hausfen, and he's almost a decade older."

There was silence in the library.

"Mother really likes Armitage, and he's offering security—"

"I wouldn't let Kevin Armitage in the same building, let alone the same room with our daughter."

Ellie had never heard her father speak with such sternness. *Kevin Armitage... That's the name on the letter yesterday at Mee-Maw's house!*

"He can get her into Oren, and she'd be more protected there."

Protected?

"I don't want to live in Oren," Elijah interrupted. A sigh followed his intrusion. "I'm sorry, Kimberly. I didn't mean to snap. I just... I really feel like everything I've said the last few years doesn't matter because you're just going to side with your mother."

"That's not true," Kimberly countered defensively.

Another moment of silence.

"Your mother will do anything to get into Oren," Elijah said calmly. "But I will *not* sacrifice our daughter for her greed and ego."

"Sacrifice?" Ellie whispered to Louie whose teeth bared at the notion of the word.

"But the prophecy," Kimberly interjected.

Ellie's eyes got wider, and she leaned harder against the vent.

"Kim, I love our life here." A floorboard squeaked. "I love our freedom."

Louie pulled his head away from the vent and looked at the back of the chair. "Mee-Maw's coming."

Damn it. Ellie pulled herself from the vent and scurried off to her room. The moment she stepped inside, Louie sounded the alarm.

"Awooo!"

"Thank you," Ellie called out and hurried off toward the front door. She joined Louie at his side. *Showtime.*

The library door opened, and Elijah's pink-cheeked face appeared. He flashed a welcoming smile. "Hey, sweetie."

"Look alive," Ellie said, and she tried to put on a fake smile even though all she wanted to do was ask about their conversation.

Kimberly hurried out of the library with her head held low. She looked like a puppy who had been scolded. "Dog! Wine," she snapped, and Louie hurried to attention.

That jerk. Ellie rounded about, ready to strike.

"Nope, not now." Elijah stopped his daughter with a hand to her lower back.

"She's picking—"

"Not now, Ellie." Elijah stopped at the small mirror that hung by the key rack. He tucked a long strand of hair behind his ear and adjusted his low ponytail.

Outside, the wooden cane sounded against the steps.

"Pamela," Elijah said as he opened the door to Mee-Maw. "Happy Friday."

"Elijah! Good to see you. You're looking well." They exchanged a kiss on the cheek. "When are you ever going to cut that hair?"

Pamela Keller-Wagner was a thin, hunched-over woman with years and years of wrinkles from frowns, grimaces, and snarls. These days, the whack of a clumsy cane and her knack for perfectly pointed pettiness were her weapons of choice. She wielded her age and frailness as a shield for pity. In the end, a dragon, no matter how old, is still a dragon.

"That gets funnier every time you say it." Elijah didn't even pretend to sound amused anymore.

"Dad's hair is gorgeous," Ellie chimed in.

"Ellie-Lynne, my darling granddaughter, always so kind." Mee-Maw pinched Ellie's cheeks to appraise her. Her smile faded. "Why do you look so exhausted? Are you not sleeping? Not eating?"

"She's eating plenty," Kimberly called back from the kitchen just as the oven beeped.

"That's me." Ellie took advantage of the call and hurried toward the kitchen as if the lasagna might become unruly if she kept it waiting.

Elijah showed the slow-moving, seventy-three-year-old woman into the dining room—not that Pamela needed the escort, but Elijah was, first and foremost, a gentleman.

"So kind of you to walk an old lady to her chair. You know Jacob never helps like this."

"Is that so?" Elijah politely replied.

"He lives a tenth of a mile away, and he can never come to see his mother?" She shook her head disapprovingly. "Little Thomas comes by to mow my lawn for me. Now, that's a proper young lad. He's getting fat, though."

Elijah pulled out the chair for her. A glass of red wine sat at each of the adult's seats. There were four chairs, four place settings, and not even a pillow or off-colored bowl in the dining room for Louie.

"Lasagna's going to need some time to cool," Ellie called out from the kitchen.

"And Ellie-Lynne," Mee-Maw continued with her assessment of the grandchildren. "Always making dinner and my arthritis lotion. Now, that's a proper young lady. She will make a man happy one day."

Kimberly popped around the corner and placed the big bowl of salad in the center of the table. "Oh, the potion-lotion. That's right! Let me get that for you, Mother."

While Kimberly fluttered away in a rush, Elijah placed a serving of salad on everyone's salad plate.

Ellie could see her mother buzz into the pantry, then poke her head out with a confused expression. She held the large jar of blue liquid and raised her eyebrows. Ellie gave her a wide smile and a big thumbs up.

"Ellie-Lynne," Kimberly muttered and shook her head as if this added some layer of stress to her night. "Looks like Ellie made you a double batch," Kimberly called out as she returned to the dining room.

Morbid curiosity had Ellie's interest, so she hung out on the other side of the kitchen wall and listened in. Louie sat between her feet.

"Why so much? You think I need this much? I'm just one old lady," Mee-Maw said.

"Pamela," Elijah began softly. "I believe the last time you were here, you mentioned how much pain you were in."

"I'm always in pain. Just getting out of bed is painful."

"Perhaps the lotion could help with that," Kimberly said. The glass jar scraped against the table as it exchanged hands.

"If I didn't know any better..." Mee-Maw began.

Ellie knew this move; she had seen it a thousand times. She closed her eyes tightly. *Come on, Mom. Resist the urge. Don't do it.*

"What's that, Mother?"

Kimberly's voice made Ellie suck frustrated air between her teeth as she winced.

"It's nothing."

"No, no, go on." Kimberly couldn't help herself.

"I was just saying... if I didn't know any better, I'd think Ellie-Lynne made such a large amount, so I wouldn't need to come back next week."

"No, no, not at all. Of course, we want you around."

"Then why is she hiding out in the kitchen? Can't even come say 'hello.' You know, I won't be around much longer. When's the last time she came for a visit? It's like I have leprosy or something. Gods be so merciful, and just take me quickly in my sleep."

"Ellie, will you stop fussing over the lasagna and keep your grandmother company?" Kimberly called out.

Ellie's cheeks turned warm as the heat of the nonexistent spotlight beat down on her from the empty kitchen. *Ugh, now I have to entertain, too.* "Sure, just let me grab the bread," Ellie called out after she took a few cautionary steps away from the wall. She didn't want to give herself away.

"I will get the bread." Kimberly moved toward the kitchen when Mee-Maw's hand caught her forearm.

"No, the Familiar should be serving us, not lying around like a useless lump. It has a job to do!"

"Yes, yes, you are right," Kimberly called out. "Louie, will you please bring in the bread?"

"You don't have to *ask* him," Mee-Maw added.

"You know if we don't ask, Ellie will be upset," Kimberly reminded her.

"That's because you haven't taught her properly. She's nineteen and unmarried. This house, it's like you want me to be a laughingstock in Oren."

Ellie let out a slow breath to calm herself. Mee-Maw's nagging and undermining were worse than ever tonight. She kneeled down with the basket of fresh bread and held out the handle for Louie to take it in his mouth.

"She's old, and she'll never change," Ellie whispered. "You're not my servant. You're my best friend, and I love you dearly. You know that, right?"

"I know. You don't need to apologize for them." Louie took the basket in his teeth, and Ellie gave him a kiss on top of the head.

They walked into the dining room, and Ellie saw that Kimberly's cheeks were just as pink as Ellie's cheeks felt.

"There she is." Kimberly looked grateful to have the focus shifted off her for a moment.

Louie hurried around the table to serve the bread.

"Where's Louie's bowl?" Ellie asked.

"Servants don't eat in the same room as—" Mee-Maw started.

"We've talked about this," Ellie snapped.

"Oh!" Mee-Maw tried to sound like a helpless, offended old woman. She held a gnarled hand over her gaping mouth.

Oh, I won't fall for your old schtick this time, Pam.

"Kimberly, I don't know why your child thinks she can speak to me in such a way. You know who has never snapped at me? Megan."

Classic Mee-Maw. Bring up the golden child. Ellie looked at her father. He closed his eyes and let out a slow, deliberate exhale. *No one? Really?*

Louie's nails clacked in Elijah's direction. "Thank you, Louie. Oh, would you look at that bow tie?" Elijah sounded genuinely happy to see him. "You're looking absolutely dapper, sir."

Over the years, Elijah had created his own subtle means of protesting Louie's mistreatment by taking every opportunity to compliment Louie and undermine Mee-Maw's bigotry.

Ellie took her regular seat at the dining room table. Down at her feet, Louie sat with big brown eyes that looked up to her lovingly. *He's willing to give up a hot meal and his place at the table, and I can't even stand up for him to an old woman?*

Ellie excused herself from the table and walked out of the dining room.

"She can't even stand my presence for a minute," Mee-Maw complained loudly.

"Sorry, mom," Ellie whispered. She brushed crumbs off of the cutting board her mom used to cut the bread. With oven mitts in hand, Ellie placed the hot, heavy, stone lasagna pan on top of it and lugged it into the dining room. "Excuse me," she announced as she made her way to the table.

Elijah quickly moved the salad bowl to make way for the large serving dish. Ellie's hands shook with the weight of it as she leaned over the table. "Careful, it's hot."

"What are you doing, Ellie?" Mee-Maw spoke with a mouth full of salad. "We aren't finished with our salads."

"This is just more convenient for me." Ellie casually discarded her oven mitts in the middle of the dining room. They clapped on the wooden floor, and she rounded the table. The wooden feet of the chair scraped against the floor as Ellie pulled it out, took her seat, and assumed her preferred, comfortable position with her legs crossed.

"That's hardly proper." Mee-Maw's nostrils flared.

Ellie scootched forcefully forward with a loud hop. She could feel Kimberly's disapproving eyes on her, but she didn't care.

Now, the coup de grace. "Come on." Ellie gave Louie a head nod and patted her lap.

Fearlessly, he hopped up into her lap.

The table fell silent.

"Corner piece?" Ellie asked Louie. The corner piece with the burned bits of cheese was Louie's favorite.

"What are you doing?" Kimberly hissed from across the table, but Ellie paid her no heed.

"Oh, yes, please!" Louie performed his Happy-Paw Dance in her lap.

Ellie reached over her salad plate to grab the serving spatula from the center of the lasagna pan, but in an instant, Mee-Maw raised her cane to strike Ellie.

Louie jumped onto the table between Pamela and Ellie. He held the wooden cane between his jaws, and his fierce eyes rested on the wielder, Pamela Keller-Wagner.

He didn't growl, and he didn't bare his teeth. For Louie, was *not* a dog. He was the offspring of fate and magic, and no one—not even a family member or a friend would lay a finger on his Ellie.

The tension in the air was thick, like the cheese in the lasagna. Everyone sat in shock at the sight before them. The only sound to break the silence was Kimberly's breath as she trembled.

"Dang, buddy! I've never seen you move like that." Ellie patted his side.

"Not. Smart," Mee-Maw hissed between her teeth. The old woman tried to pull her cane back, but Louie held it in place.

Elijah cleared his throat. "Louie, would you please return to your seat?"

Louie held Mee-Maw in his gaze for a moment longer, sank his teeth harder into the cane so the wood whined, and finally released it. He hopped back into Ellie's lap. Then, with a flick of Elijah's wrist, the basket of bread floated from Kimberly's side of the table and settled beside Ellie and Louie's plate.

"Ellie." Elijah's voice was calm and collected. His words were properly enunciated, and his cheeks were pink. "Would you please make yours and Louie's plates and eat in your room? We need to speak with your grandmother."

"Dad, I'm not a child."

"Would you please humor me?" Elijah didn't take his eyes off Mee-Maw.

"Okay." As Ellie took two slices of bread, Louie hopped off her lap and started toward the bedroom.

"Louie." Elijah caught his attention before the Familiar could leave the room. With another flick of Elijah's wrist, the breadbasket lifted from the table and purposefully glided through the air. It came to a stop just before the basset hound's jaws. "A feat of such bravery earns more than a single slice of bread."

Louie's tail wagged with excitement. He accepted the basket handle between his teeth and waddled toward their room.

Everything remained silent and tense until Ellie shut her bedroom door. Of course, the curious duo sat on the other side and listened in. Elijah's voice was low, but thankfully, when he was angry, he enunciated his words and spoke slowly.

"I warned you," he began.

"Me?" Mee-Maw sounded surprised. "I was the victim here—"

"I'm speaking!" Elijah's voice thundered through the door. "I told you that if you ever raised your hand to *my* daughter, or yours, for that matter, you would not be welcomed back."

"Elijah—" Kimberly tried interrupting.

"No, Kimberly. We agreed."

The room fell silent again.

"Pamela, you need to leave," Elijah said loudly and sternly.

"Elijah Becker." Mee-Maw's tone had all the sweetness of white vinegar. "You're willing to cut off the oldest member of the Keller-Wagner family, to lose it all over some lasagna?"

"This is Becker land," he reminded her. "You have no rights here. You need to leave."

"Fine. Send an old lady home without supper." Mee-Maw's chair scraped against the ground. "Don't be surprised if I fall and break a hip. Then, the bears will eat me on my way home."

The cane clacked against the floor slowly, rhythmically, dissipating down the hallway. The screen door screeched open, then slammed shut on the overly enthusiastic hinges.

7

Sharing

Tension lingered in the air even after Mee-Maw left. Ellie and Louie kept to their room until they were certain Kimberly had gone to bed.

"Are you sure he'll be up for talking after everything?" Louie asked as Ellie pulled a baggy sweater over her pajamas.

"I don't know; he seemed pretty angry," she admitted and pulled the clip out of her hair. "But the worst thing he can say is 'no,' right?"

Many years ago, Elijah had finished the garage with insulation, sheetrock, and a coat of robin's-egg blue paint. It was his safe haven, his workshop. Kimberly and Ellie added the finishing touches to make him feel right at home.

Enjoy the magic of this lovely workspace.
Love, Kim
EB&EB Garage-where anything can happen!

A paw print in black ink accompanied the note.

Very rarely was there actually a car parked in the well-organized garage. The cement floor was usually populated with one of Elijah's many projects, which ranged from small engine repair to woodworking. His coveted project sat off to the side, covered with a dark-blue tarp, but Ellie knew better than to ask him what was underneath it again. The one time she did, he turned to her with a smirk and said, "That's classified."

Tonight, classic rock played softly from the radio perched on a shelf. The garage smelled of motor oil, and Elijah sat at his workbench with a small, dense metal object in his hand. He inspected it with careful eyes under a large, bright work lamp clamped onto the edge of the desk.

Ellie and Louie broke his concentration as his lips moved along subconsciously to the familiar tune that played over the radio. "There's the hero of the evening," Elijah said, welcoming them.

The wrinkly basset hound hopped down the wooden garage steps with all the grace of a well-loved plastic slinky.

Louie's head raised with pride as he walked over to Elijah and took a seat at his feet. Ellie pulled up an old plastic egg crate.

The sight of her father working on a project brought Ellie back to her childhood, when her father would sneak cookies from the cookie jar so that he and Ellie could have a 'midnight snack' in the garage. In reality, their little dates occurred well before midnight, and her dad always ushered her out and tucked her into bed by eleven, at the latest.

"Seeing you working like this made me get one heck of a sweet tooth," Ellie declared.

"Ahhh. Our midnight snacks. Yeah. Those were the days." A pleasant, distant memory floated through his eyes. "So, what brings you in?"

The words Ellie had rehearsed in her head refused to come out. "I uh... well... something happened today..."

Elijah turned down the radio.

"While making the potion-lotion."

"Yeah. You didn't ask me to help this time. How was it doing it by yourself?"

"I wasn't alone. Louie helped me."

"Oh?" Elijah placed the project on his workstation. She had his full, undivided attention now.

"You know when we channel the Void?"

He nodded.

"I think we went deeper."

Elijah's eyes fluttered between Ellie and Louie, and he stroked his mustache with his oily hand. He realized his mistake immediately and wiped his hands and mustache on an old rag. "Well, go on, sweetheart. What was it like?"

"Weird," she said. "There was a Seer and..."

Elijah's eyes opened wide.

"It was like fifty of them talking to us at once." Ellie's hands gestured towards her body.

"There was just one," Louie reassured her.

Ellie looked down at Louie. "What?"

"There was just one Seer."

"Oh," Ellie said. "It felt like a lot of different voices coming at me, all at one time."

Elijah picked up his flat, rectangular carpenter's pencil and jotted a note on a scrap of paper. "Continue."

Ellie revisited the story she had been playing over and over in her head. When she was done, Ellie stared at her father, waiting for a response, but Elijah said nothing. She could see the gears turning in his mind as he reviewed things he had jotted down on the paper.

Finally, he said, "Fascinating."

"Really? That's it?"

"This is uncharted territory for me, my dear. Remember, it's been a long time since a Familiar showed up in either of our families. I think the last one for the Beckers was... maybe six generations ago?"

"Why so long?"

"I think you're asking the wrong guy." Elijah gestured towards Louie, who had laid down on the concrete floor with his stomach up towards the ceiling.

"I don't have all the answers, either," Louie said. "I told you before, there's a lot left up to chance, Ellie. Before I found you, it wasn't just me up there. Hundreds of us raced toward Earth, and after landing, I wandered around the Void for a long time before I found your Seer."

"I know, I know. Lots of dust, lots of mirror puddles," Ellie said.

"Dust?" Elijah asked.

"Piles of ash," Louie clarified. "Stars who burned out waiting at the wrong puddle."

Burned out. Ellie turned to Louie.

Ellie's gaze softened. *Ohhh.* The Void wasn't just the birthplace of magic; it was a tomb for Seers and other creatures of darkness. *It's a graveyard.*

"I could've ended up walking around until I lost all power and burnt out—that is if I was lucky enough to burn out. Otherwise, I could've become corrupted by loneliness." Louie shivered. "Luckily, I found my guide, my friend, Seer. She showed me what my life could be, what her life was. She took me to you and, well, you know the rest."

"I don't know the rest," Elijah said, leaning forward expectantly.

"Oh! Oh!" Ellie excitedly picked the pup up and put him onto her lap. "Story time requires cuddles."

Louie nuzzled Ellie before retelling his story. "The new moon preceding Ellie's birth was the day I was, well, born. All of us shooting stars who fell towards Earth got twisted up in the magic, and we came to life. We raced one another towards these doorways, these slits that invited us into the Void."

Louie put his weight back into his hindquarters and lifted his front paws up.

"I can remember this one other shooting star beside me that had its eyes on that slit. I think my weight helped me get the speed I needed, the edge against it."

As Louie talked, his paws came closer together.

"You see, only one of us can get through into the Void. The moment you pass through, the doorway disappears. Those who don't make it burn up in the atmosphere."

Elijah's mouth dropped open, but he didn't interrupt Louie.

"I entered with such speed, I was out of control, and I managed to run straight into a large rock." He demonstrated by smacking his paws together. "When I came to, I was lying on the ground and looking up. I could see the universe before me—the stars, the galaxies, the planets. It was breathtaking, and I could have laid there for a long time in awe, but something was calling to me."

"The Seer?" Elijah softly questioned.

"I don't think so." Louie shook his head as he tried to think back. "When a Seer calls to you, it's like a voice that reverberates inside of you, but this was more like a yearning. I think it was Ellie."

"She wasn't born yet." Elijah gestured with the pencil.

"Time doesn't work the same way there," Ellie said, repeating Louie's earlier point.

The pup nodded and muttered. "But more than that, my love for Ellie—the connection I have to her—well, it's beyond reason and rhyme."

Louie let that hang in the air a moment before he continued.

"Anyway, I couldn't shoot off through the Void. Something kept me grounded, and somehow, I managed to form legs. Then, I began the long, lonely walk to find what was calling to me. With no sun and no day, I can't really estimate how long I walked before I saw my first Familiar. They leaned over a shimmering pool and watched their wizard as he ran around."

"They?" Elijah asked.

"The Familiar and the Seer," Louie reminded him. "It's nearly impossible to find your puddle without your Seer."

"Ah! The guide during potions?" Ellie asked.

"Exactly. As odd as Seers may seem, they understand the Void. After dedicating their entire afterlife to it, they know it intimately. They become one with it—or at least that's what she told me."

"The Seer is a 'she'?" Ellie pulled Louie back to look at her.

"Let's tackle that later, Ellie." Elijah made a note. "I really want to hear the rest of this."

Louie licked Ellie's cheek before he returned to his story. "So, I left them alone and went on to find Ellie. I came across dozens of dead, lifeless pools—and piles of ash."

"You said that the piles of ash were burned-out shooting stars?" Elijah's pencil gestured to his twirling thoughts in the air.

"Yes. Stars like me. They either stayed too long at the wrong pool or never found it," Louie confirmed.

"That's why you needed to find your Seer," Ellie added.

"Correct."

"So, how did you find Seer?" Elijah asked.

"She was singing." Louie looked off in the distance as he hummed the jazzy tune for them.

"That's my song," Ellie said defensively.

"Well, that's the song that led me to Seer, who took me to you." Louie continued. "She was off in her own world, so I threw a rock at her to get her attention. Then, together, we walked through the Void until we came upon your puddle. I believe we made it with two days to spare before you were born."

"So, you sat there in front of the puddle until the ceremony?" Elijah's pencil tapped against his fingertips.

"Yep. Until Ellie needed me." Louie nodded. "Then, Seer kicked me, so I came down."

"She kicked you?" Ellie chuckled.

"Yes, if I remember correctly, I was... sparking." Louie made an explosive gesture with his hands. "I was furious about that man—that creepy guy from the veggie platter."

Louie looked like he was struggling with his memory.

"He, uh, he kept eyeballing you, and I was so angry. Then... well, Seer gave me the boot, and that's why I landed in the food instead of next to you."

Ellie stifled her laughter into the back of Louie's head.

Elijah sat back in his tall work chair and tapped the edge of the pencil against his mustache. "So why a basset hound?"

"Oh, I wanted to choose a form that would make Ellie most happy."

Ellie emphasized this point by playing with his long, floppy ears. "Remember Mindy's dog?"

A jolly smile crossed Elijah's face at the memory. "You wouldn't leave that poor old thing alone. Smart choice, Louie. So, you could've turned into anything? A cat? A leopard? A manatee?"

"Yep."

"You mean you could have turned into a hermit crab?" Ellie added reproachfully and stopped playing with his ears.

Louie bobbed his head back in protest until she started playing with them again. "I will be whatever you need me to be." He sighed. "As much as we adore hermit crabs, I don't see the practical use for one in your day-to-day life. Try to imagine one of those scrubbing the floor with you."

Ellie played with his paws and made scrubbing motions. Louie patiently endured her silliness.

Elijah broke the silence. "You're a good friend."

"Best friend." Ellie stopped harassing Louie and set his paws on her knees.

With that, he hopped down and returned to the space on the cold cement floor between Ellie and Elijah.

"Why is mom so mean to him?" Ellie blurted out.

"*That* is a conversation for you to have with her," Elijah replied.

"Can you talk to her, though?" Ellie asked sheepishly. "Like, try to convince her to be more respectful?"

"If you can't stand up to your mother, then how'll you stand up to a boss or a friend who oversteps?"

Ellie sighed. That was always her father's argument. "A boss? I can barely go to the grocery store without Mom having a fit. How would I get a job—"

"Again, you have to talk to her about that. You know my stance on all of this."

Ellie's shoulders slumped with defeat.

"I want to circle back," Elijah said, redirecting the conversation. "Louie, regarding Seer. You mentioned that she showed you her life?"

"Yes," Louie confirmed.

"Have you shared this with Kim?"

Louie shook his head from side to side.

"Would you be willing to?"

"Yeah. Maybe they could sit at the table and have coffee and cookies." Ellie's sarcasm hung thick in the air.

"I understand she has been difficult, but I think speaking to her about this could go far in building up a relationship based on trust," Elijah said, staring at Ellie.

This is pointless, Ellie thought. It wasn't like she hadn't tried to speak with her mother before. Every time she brought up the way her mother spoke to Louie, she would just double down or change the subject. But, for her father, she would give it one last try. She smiled and nodded at him.

"Anything else I can help you with, my dear Ellie?"

Elijah was never one to end a conversation early, but with the bags under his eyes and the mess on the bench, Ellie knew he was running out of steam. Still, it was rare for her to get one-on-one time with her father like this.

"I heard you and mom talking today," she said quietly.

Elijah's expression softened.

"Dad, I don't want an arranged marriage."

Elijah sighed and dropped his hand onto the workbench. His eyes searched the floor between them. "I hear you, honey, and I know this is important to talk about, but can we table this for another night? I don't have it in me tonight."

Ellie's shoulders slumped.

"I promise—you and me, tomorrow night?"

Ellie glanced at Louie, and he gave her a gentle nod.

"Alright," she said in defeat. "You'll bring the cookies?"

"It's a deal."

They shook on it.

Ellie and Louie made their way back to the bedroom and snuggled up beneath the covers. A chilly spring breeze from the slightly open window danced over Ellie's face. The smell of dampness, pollen, and wood filled her nose. Louie lay with his head across her chest and his nose against the bottom of her chin. Ellie gently stroked his long, velvety ears, though they couldn't soothe her into a peaceful sleep. Dread filled her chest as she thought about her discussion with her father.

"Mom's not going to listen, is she?" Ellie mumbled.

"Try to be open-minded. If you go in with that headspace, you may condemn her before she has a chance to change—like a self-fulfilling prophecy."

Prophecy. Ellie completely forgot to ask her father about that. She put the heels of her palms to her forehead and let out a frustrated groan. "Crap!"

Everything about this was irritating.

Why should I have to wait? It's my life! Just because they gave into an arranged marriage doesn't mean that I have to. Don't I get some sort of say? Can't I decline? Decline, decline, decline. I will say 'no' to every last one of them, and then what?

Ellie tossed and turned through hours of Louie snoring and reruns of sitcoms on the television behind her. The gentle breeze from the open window did little to cool her head.

Can't even be nice to my Familiar? Just keep pushing and pushing. See where that'll get you, Mom. Siding with that awful woman. Keeping crap from me. I'm an adult. I can make my own choices now. Normal people my age get to run off to college or get their own apartment. I can't even go into all the rooms of the house—especially the stupid library.

With her back to Louie, Ellie crossed her arms and stared at the wall. Her map of the United States with a pushpin in the upper right-hand corner of Connecticut taunted her.

Talk to her. Like I haven't tried a zillion times? Ellie turned over again, and her heavy eyes landed on the alarm clock, which read 2:21a.m. *Ah-hhhh!*

She threw one of her pillows to the floor. Louie sat up for a moment, saw that there was no danger, and laid his fat head back down.

That stupid library. She glared at the ceiling. *You know what? She can't stop me from going into it while she's sleeping, can she?*

Ellie eased out of bed, and with determined, quiet steps, she hurried out of her room down the hall. She paused in front of the most secretive, sacred room in the house—the library.

8

The Library

The first time Ellie was allowed in her mother's coveted library was for her assignment on Magic and Genealogy—one of Kimberly's self-taught and 'oh-so-important classes.' Ellie stood in front of the family tree, copied it, and tried to trace magical lineages with different colored pencils. That led to a lecture on genetics, something about green beans and cross-breeding, and then to how she got her mother's blue eyes instead of her father's dominant brown eyes.

"Mom, is magic a recessive trait?" Ellie had asked. "Is that why you don't have a mark?"

"Yes, that's why." Kimberly swallowed hard and left the room as quickly as a mouse scurrying from a cat.

According to Lianne, another theory that bounced between family members- that Kimberly was the product of an affair with a delivery driver from Oren.

Tonight, against the soft moonlight, the library looked unchanged. The large, comfortable armchair still sat near the center of the room, before the window, with the medium-sized rug Ellie had made for her mom before it. The small, pine end table sat along the left-hand side of the armchair with a notepad, a coaster, and an ancient carrying case full of pencils.

Ellie grumbled as she took in the pristine, organized room. Not a speck of dust. It was petty, but Ellie swapped the notepad and the coaster. She stuck her tongue out at the table as if her mother would receive the message.

This small jab brought a pleased, devilish smile to Ellie's lips that only lasted for a brief moment as she noticed an annotation in the notebook. Ellie took a seat in the chair and made a point to lay her leg over the arm.

Ouroboros-Hogwash

The previous pages easily flipped over the rings of the top-bound miniature notebook, and Ellie worked backward through her mother's passive thoughts for the past few weeks. *Gimme something about an arranged marriage.* Of course, the most recent entries were all about snakes and water snakes.

Werewolf curse-genetic?

Ellie raised her eyebrows. That thought had never crossed her mind before. *Up to some weird research in here.* According to family rumors, Aunt Kelly's twin ran off with a werewolf boy to avoid an arranged marriage when they were younger. *I don't blame her. I'll take a werewolf over grandpas any day.*

3TaRX

The weird cluster of letters and numbers didn't soothe Ellie's arched brow.

Gatineau Park-Missing couple hiking and canoeing
-Wechuge? See 9We2018X.
-Werewolf? See 9Wo2012X.

Gatineau? Ellie's eyebrows furrowed together. *That sounds so familiar. Wait, is she trying to find Aunt Jean?*

Frantically, Ellie flipped back to the previous page, looking for some clues to validate her suspicion, but there was nothing—only another set of letters and numbers.

Thunderbird—mentioned across many indigenous cultures.
See 1AlRX, 1OjRX, and 1GrRx.

The letters must be a code. Of course, she'd have a code.

Ellie walked over to the first shelving unit closest to the desk. On the top row, she saw "0WiRX," so she pulled it from the shelf. The book read "Wicca: The New Aged Witch."

Ellie put it back and skipped a few shelves, where the first number on the spines changed. Finally, she pulled the book labeled 1AlRX from the shelf—"Algonquin Legends." Ellie opened the book and thumbed through a few pages. Eventually, she found a piece of paper tucked between the pages like a temporary bookmark, and on that page, a passage about the great Thunderbird was underlined in pencil.

Ellie tossed the book onto the desk and searched through the shelf for 1OjRX, "Ojibwe: Legends, Lessons and Spiritual Beliefs." She held that book aside and selected the next one, which a very small. On second glance, it looked like an article Kimberly had printed, self-bound, and coded—"Great Sun and His Messengers-Menominee 1GrRx."

"Algonquin... Ojibwe... Those are indigenous tribes," Ellie whispered. She held the books side by side so she could look at the tags and titles. "Al... Oj... the first two letters of the names. R? Rx?" Ellie shuffled the books and studied the shelves, trying to decipher the code. "What does R mean?"

Ellie paced the length of the shelves as she examined other codes and titles.

Brothers Grimm-5BrRX

Collection of Greek Tragedies-3CoRX

None of this made sense. There was a theme with the first number, like a way to categorize them, then the name of the title, but the last two letters made no sense to her. She walked back up the length of the bookshelves, past the window, and toward the desk. It hit her.

"Of course." She rushed forward and searched through the desk drawers, but she saw no sign of letters, sticky notes, or anything that mentioned an arranged marriage or prophecy. However, smack-dab in the middle of the main drawer, she found a laminated, handwritten index card:

0-*Modern practices and interpretations*
1-*Western hemisphere, Indigenous cultures*
2-*Eastern Hemisphere, Indigenous cultures*
3-*Roman, Greek, and Egyptian Ancient Religions*
4-*African Folklore*
5-*European Folklore*
6-*Wars, Genocide, and Religious Oppression*
7-*Lunar Studies, the Stars and Space*
8-*Autobiographies, Journals, and other Primary Sources*
9-*Kimberly's Personal Journals, Theories, and Conclusions*

Following their category, the first three letters of the title,
not to include the words The, A or An.
If personal journal, the year it was written.

R = Read
X = Cross-Referenced
H = Hogwash

"H for Hogwash?" Ellie's eyebrows pulled together judgmentally. "She thinks she's British?"

Now that she had the formula for the codes, it made finding the sections she wanted much easier. She decided to start with 9We2018X.

Personal Journal of Kimberly Lynne Keller-Wagner Becker,
Daughter of Pamela Keller-Wagner and Alfred Keller.

Born June 23, 1963
Married: Elijah Becker
Daughter: Ellie-Lynne Becker* Familiar, Louie

Ellie turned the page to what looked like a title page.

A Study of the Notorious Wendigo

Before I begin, please note that Wendigo is a popular name given to a terrifying creature of the night. The name "Wendigo" is the Algonquin name for it. It is my belief that this creature does, in fact, exist. Through the following pages and referenced material, I will prove my case. I do believe the Wendigo is a bipedal, man-eating creature often associated with witches and sorcery.

The next page contained a crudely drawn illustration. Thankfully, Ellie did not inherit her artistic skills from her mother. The blobs were labeled—Quebec, New England, Washington, Oregon, New Mexico, and Arizona—which was the only reason Ellie knew it was a map.

A pencil line divided the subsequent page into two halves. The indigenous names were on the left, while the meanings or descriptions of the creatures were on the right.

Skin Walkers "yee Naaldlooshii" (Navajo)	*Witch and shapeshifter*
Ghost Witch "Skadegamutc" (Abenaki)	*Witch, undead, cannibal, drinks blood*
Wendigo (First Peoples with Multiple Names)	*Cannibalistic, bipedal*

Ellie closed the book and put it back. She pulled through a few more journals:

9Th2016X
Personal Journal of Kimberly Lynne Keller-Wagner Becker, Daughter of Pamela Keller-Wagner and Alfred Keller.

Born June 23, 1963
Married: Elijah Becker
Daughter: Ellie-Lynne Becker* Familiar, Louie

A Study of Thunderbird

She glared at the asterisk before she put back the book. *Nobody wants to read your diaries, Kimberly. Moving on.*

9El2000X
Personal Journal of Kimberly Lynne Keller-Wagner Becker, Daughter of Pamela Keller-Wagner and Alfred Keller.
Born June 23, 1963
Married: Elijah Becker
Daughter: Ellie-Lynne Betty Becker* Familiar, Louie
A Biography of my Beloved Daughter, Ellie-Lynne Betty Becker

That's more like it. Curious, Ellie took a seat back on the floor. "Show me what you've got, Kimberly."

> *Ellie was born on October 16th, 2000. It was a natural birth that lasted many painful hours. She was born in our New England farmhouse at the hands of my mother, Pamela Keller-Wagner. Mother was not a trained nurse, but the circumstances of Ellie's birth were complicated and difficult. We did what we could on that cold October night.*
>
> *Ellie was a smart child-*

And she hates reading about herself. She skipped ahead a few pages to the Becoming Ceremony, to Louie's introduction to her life.

October 2013

It was a lovely ceremony! The heaters worked perfectly and kept everyone comfortable. Every family member invited showed up, and we even had suitors interested despite her minor ability.

During the ceremony, Ellie was blessed with a Familiar. He arrived in the form of a basset hound that looked remarkably similar to the basset hound of her childhood friend. He landed in the center of the food table, created a humongous mess, and, of course, Ellie fell instantly in love with him. That would make sense as a Familiar takes the form that will most please their Master—See 8Ah1656X.

Awkwardly, Ellie kept her eyes on the page as she got up and rushed over to the pine end table so she could write down the reference number. Ahren Wagner was the last known person in her family to have a Familiar before her. He was also the reason Ellie's family immigrated to the Americas back in the early 1600s to escape the witch trials in Europe.

According to Ahren Wagner, a Familiar is a servant meant to obey their Master and their Master's family. It is a magical creature made to ward off other magical creatures and to fight to the death for its Master.

Louie quickly became a member of our family, though. He was like the pet dog we never had. When Ellie attended class, he would respect her time and keep her focused. When she was allowed to play, they would run through the gardens and forest together. He may not be the protector Aksel (Ahren's Familiar) acted as, but he brings her joy.

January, 2014

It is the New Year following Ellie's Becoming Ceremony. As is tradition, she has begun potion lessons with her father. Ellie has quickly taken to her lessons and has become proficient with the basic soothing potion, resting potion, calming potion, and itch remedy. Those are typical starter potions for all families, as they are mono-herbal recipes and require significantly less power, as chamomile is such a powerful herb in itself. Elijah will lead family morning meditations to get Ellie into the habit so she has an ever-present connection with The Void. It brings me such pride to see her excel! This coming year she will take on the full responsibility of the garden, from soil preparation through harvest. We will also move her forward in her Foraging lessons into the more complex realm of fungus. I do hope that old birch is still producing healthy amounts of chaga.

February, 2014

Ellie's lessons continue without issue. She is difficult to wake in the morning, but once she gets into the living room with her father, she does assume her best behavior. The Familiar is a peculiar creature. The way a Familiar has been described by Ahren Wagner (8Ah1656X) is barely reflective of Louie.

Ahren's Familiar was "so quiet, one would barely know it was there until it was too late." Louie is like a clumsy freight train. I can't help but wonder where the difference lies. Ahren often mentioned his Familiar spent time protecting the house from critters like mice, rats, and bats.

Louie seems more docile—I thought this stage would be only temporary. It will be fascinating to see firsthand how their partnership develops and unfolds.

Ellie made another note of Ahren Wagner's book number.

March, 2014

Spring is beginning in Connecticut. Ellie has planted the seedlings for this year's garden in the greenhouse, and they will be transplanted in the months to follow. The Familiar seems to be taking on a more traditional role when there is work to be done—digging at the dirt and bringing Ellie the tools she needs.

The way they interact does not sound much like Ahren's description. Ahren often boasted of Aksel's devotion, which is true of Louie, but I worry that if someone were to attack Ellie, this little basset hound could not stand its ground against them, like when Aksel took down the witch hunters.

A basset hound may be easier to get around in modern society as opposed to a full-grown adult black bear. But then again, with Ellie staying within Connecticut, within our society, a witch hunter wouldn't be able to find her, anyway. So, what is the need for a Familiar these days? I speculate, but perhaps his form and his docile nature are the results of a strong and safe foundation that Ahren laid out for us.

Ellie has completed her readings of The Brothers Grimm, a collection of Western European Folklore. She will begin reading collections of similar stories from other cultures. I cannot wait! I hope her curiosity is sparked like mine was and she begins down the road of research.

April, 2014

The garden is coming along nicely. It is with the heaviest heart I share that I found mention of Ellie in the writings of Betty Fischer (8Be1945RX).

I do not believe I could really call it a "journal," but a collection of insane ramblings. I find it difficult to record this as an impartial third party. I am sick just writing it, but Betty predicted Ellie's death.

As her parent, I am enraged that this leach of a Familiar has lived under our roof for years! I knew such a docile form was a mistake! I detest his false promises to keep Ellie safe. He is meant to put his life before hers. And I despise him for not fulfilling his duties.
May Ahren's soul curse him.

"8Be1945," Ellie muttered the reference number as she dropped the biography and scrambled back to the shelf. "8Be1945. 8Be1945."

Predicted Ellie's death. The words persisted through her thoughts, and her hands trembled as she reached for the shelf.

The journal was old, and the binding was cracked. Chunks of the dull, worn leather were missing, and the thread on the edges threatened to come loose. Ellie tried to handle the book delicately, but her shaking fingers betrayed her. She flipped through the pages in an attempt to find a bookmark, a dog-eared page, anything to find the prophecy. Finally, Ellie noticed a bright-blue sticky note with her mother's script in the upper right-hand corner: EBB.

A creature of darkness, of hunger, of longing, and suffering—a Familiar—lost and alone.
Ellie-Lynne Betty Becker will meet her fate one spring eve.
Pain and temptation.
The Void calls.
Heat.

Ellie's tired eyes read over the words again and again. She couldn't believe what the pages said.

Ellie-Lynne Betty Becker will meet her fate one spring eve.

Exhausted, Ellie put everything back in its place except for the one journal she wanted to keep. She removed her handwritten note from the notebook and closed the shelves with her shoulders slumped over. When she returned to her room, Louie was right where she had left him a few hours ago. Eyes dry from exhaustion and her mind dull and silent, Ellie climbed into bed.

Ellie-Lynne Betty Becker will meet her fate one spring eve.

Before she could get a moment of sleep, her mother knocked on the door. "It's time to wake up."

Louie hopped on Ellie and licked her.

"No! No licking today," Ellie whined. Her head ached and was filled with a slow, heavy cloudiness. Something odd, thick, and cool sat in her hand on her chest. She had fallen asleep with Betty Fischer's journal. As quick as she could, Ellie rolled over and tucked the journal away in her bedside drawer.

"What was that?" Louie asked eagerly.

"Book." She yawned and pulled herself from bed.

"Oh? Which one?"

Ellie didn't want to explain. "Brother's Grimm."

Louie visibly cringed and turned away. "I don't like them, too scary." He hopped down off of the bed.

As they got ready for the day, Ellie dreaded her dad's special Saturday morning breakfast. "I don't want to look at Mom," Ellie grumbled as she thought of the breakfast table.

The Void calls.

9

Angel

Nineteen-year-old Elijah Becker sat on the wooden swing in the center of the old gazebo. Three weeks earlier, the canary yellow paint was chipped and even missing some planks of wood, but not to-day. In preparation for this day, the family fixed up the old structure. His mother pressed their shirts and dusted the nooks and crannies of the house. Next to his Becoming Ceremony, today was the biggest day of Elijah Becker's life.

It was mid-fall, and a few leaves clung desperately to trees, the smell of decay in the air. It was his favorite time of the year, but even on this cool, beautiful autumn day, he found his underarms, the back of his neck, and his upper lip damp with sweat.

"Oh, no." He lifted his arm so his brother, Christopher, could see. "Do I have to change my shirt again?"

"Oh, yeah." Christopher chuckled to torment his older brother.

"Switch shirts with me." Elijah had already unbuttoned the mustard shirt his mother insisted he wear.

"What?"

"Come on! She's going to be here any second! I have to make a good first impression."

Christopher, who could be Elijah's twin, rolled his eyes and pulled off his light-blue polo. "I can't believe you're going through with this."

"Like I have a choice?"

"I mean, you could always run like Matt."

Elijah hadn't heard his older brother's name in years. "You know that would push Mom into her deathbed." Elijah snagged the light-blue polo and pulled it on.

"Just saying, you're telekinetic. You could do better than someone with 'some good genes.'"

Breathe. Elijah regained his calm demeanor. As he focused his breathing, his heart rate slowed, and his thoughts calmed.

The French doors of the back porch swung open.

Oh gods. All his meditative work was undone.

Forced laughter filled the air, and an older woman with harsh wrinkles on her forehead walked out of the house.

Pamela, he swallowed hard. *Yeah, she looks as approachable as a rattlesnake.*

Elijah's mom, Edna Becker, followed the old lady. She was a cheerful, tiny little thing with white hair braided on each side of her head and pulled back into a ponytail. Thick, charming spectacles rested on her hooked nose. Edna was dressed in her best floral-patterned jumpsuit.

Ralph Becker dressed for the occasion in a white and red striped button-up, complimented by a perfect tie. He was a tall, older man with a button nose, glorious thick mustache, and eyebrows to match.

Elijah self-consciously felt his own mustache. He did everything he possibly could that morning to make sure it looked well taken care of, but it always looked pathetic when he stood next to his dad.

One day, Elijah reassured himself.

On this beautiful fall day, amongst the sweat, scrutiny, and sunshine, Elijah witnessed the emergence of an angel. Kimberly, a shy-looking young woman with a plump frame and flushed cheeks, stepped out of his parent's house and into the backyard garden. Her wavy hair was pulled up into a half-do. Beautiful blue eyes shimmered behind her glasses. All the nerves melted away.

Click, click, click, clack.

The angel floated across the stone walkway towards him. *My future wife... oh my gods... she looks so kind... so beautiful... and I'm in a stupid polo. She's smiling at me.*

His heart pounded against his chest, and the sensation in his stomach was like a battalion of butterflies.

What do I say?

The sound of his own heartbeat in his ears drowned out the clacking of her heels against the stone.

"This is my son, Eli—"

Everything around him started to go dark as his mom introduced them. His body felt heavy, and his head felt light. The last thing he remembered was the gazebo's ceiling as his consciousness left him.

"Oh no," Edna called out and rushed forward.

***

Saturday-Present Day

The sun peeked through the curtains of their bedroom, and the birds sang outside. Kimberly lay at her husband's side, her wavy locks dominating her pillow and tickling his face. With a gentle hand, he tucked the curls along her back and tenderly embraced her while she slept.

A beautiful Saturday.

Her cocoa-colored hair smelled sweet, like something fruity. It still held a beautiful, healthy shimmer despite the infiltration of her gorgeous grays.

As he lay in bed beside her, he thought of his talk with Ellie the night before. With a soft sigh, he tried to push the thoughts away. He wanted to remain present and enjoy the heat of Kimberly's skin beneath his touch, but it was no use. After ten minutes, Elijah rolled his eyes and climbed out of bed.

"Sleep well, my darling." He kissed Kimberly's forehead before he went to the bathroom. After his shower, with his thick locks tied up into a towel to dry, he combed out his mustache and delicately trimmed it.

"*Dad, I don't want an arranged marriage.*" Elijah closed his eyes and set his scissors on the white bathroom vanity. *This is going to go over like a lead balloon.*

Small white and black hairs speckled the inside of the sink basin. His stomach turned over as he thought about the impending conversation.

How do I tell her? "*Honey, our hands are tied. Just be grateful your grandma isn't the one making the decisions.*" His hand drummed the surface with frustration. *That's not the right approach.*

With a glance in the mirror, Elijah met his reflection. His eyes faltered when he tried to hold his own gaze.

The suitors, the prophecy, the needle... I'd hate me. To not face his own reflection again, Elijah focused on washing the facial hair down the drain. *And Kimmy...*

With a flick of his wrist, the towel left his hair, and the scissors returned to their spot in the cup on the shelf.

One thing at a time... just get through this morning.

The early morning light fought to fill the quaint kitchen as Elijah made coffee. He stood at the window and admired the growing garden until the coffee machine screamed at him. Just like every Saturday morning, his favorite oversized mug sat to the right of the coffee maker with a brand-new copy of *THEM Timely*—a celebrity gossip magazine. Everyone in the house had their guilty pleasure reads, and he couldn't deny it; he loved hearing the ridiculous stories about celebrities.

With a large, steaming mug in hand, Elijah sat at the dining room table and opened the magazine. For the next hour, he flipped through absurd stories, articles, and interviews with a grin on his lips.

"Oh, Stacey, you'll figure it out," he muttered as he turned another page.

When his need for coffee and silliness was satiated, he returned to the kitchen to make breakfast for his family. It wasn't long before the smell of bacon filled the house. A tower of chocolate chip pancakes was under construction when a pair of hands caressed Elijah's abdomen. All the tension in his shoulders melted with her touch.

"Good morning, Angel."

"What did I ever do to deserve such a wonderful husband?"

"You're just buttering me up to steal my bacon."

Kimberly's playful giggle filled his heart with warmth. *She has no idea how powerful that smile is.*

Her hand darted toward the crispy, fatty bacon, and Elijah wrapped his arms around her. She quickly shoved it into her mouth.

"How dare you?" he teased and kissed her neck.

She squealed with laughter. "Stop tickling! That's not fair."

With a little spin, she escaped his arms. Kimberly took Elijah by surprise when she gently slapped him with a chocolate chip pancake.

He gasped dramatically.

Their flirtatious game continued as he chased her around the kitchen. Finally, the game ended with a loving embrace by the sink.

"Good morning, my love," Kimberly said.

"Good morning," Elijah replied with a kiss to her forehead. "Go enjoy it. I'll bring you breakfast."

With a pinch to his rump, Kimberly walked to the dining room with a cup of coffee.

"No! No licking today," Ellie cried out from down the hallway.

Their morning ritual brought a smile to Elijah's face—but also a heaviness to his stomach. A small voice in the back of his head informed him this could be his last day with his small family before everything fell apart.

Breathe. He closed his eyes and exhaled slowly as bacon cracked in the pan.

"Hey, Dad." Ellie and Louie rounded the corner as he put the last pancake on the stack.

Triumphantly, Elijah raised his hands up in the air and announced. "Seventeen!"

"New record." Ellie's lack of enthusiasm and her puffy eyes didn't sit right with him. A part of him suspected she was up all-night fretting about the impending conversations. He tried to push aside his assumption.

As Ellie filled a glass full of water, Elijah leaned over toward her and dropped his tone. "You alright, kiddo?"

Ellie lazily nodded, but he wasn't buying it.

"She didn't sleep well," Louie explained.

"Good morning, Louie." As is tradition, Elijah handed him a strip of bacon.

"Oh!" Louie happily accepted it and crunched it down.

Without being asked, Ellie took the fresh pot of coffee, creamer, and sugar out to the dining room table.

"Thank you, sweetheart," he heard Kimberly say from the other room. "Oh, sweety, you look so tired."

"You're welcome," Ellie grumbled as she walked back toward the kitchen and grabbed the fixings for the pancakes.

Elijah followed with the pancakes and bacon on a large, white, ceramic serving dish.

As Saturday morning routine would have it, Kimberly sat in the shimmering morning light of the dining room with a book in hand. Outside of the library, Kimberly only read fiction—not research material. She loved fantastical romances, damsels in distress, or heroines toppling a tyrannical government.

"Oooh," Kimberly purred when she saw Elijah with the food. She closed her book.

Elijah set the tray in the center of the table and served Kimberly with a tiny stack of pancakes, the warmest, freshest ones. Ellie refilled Kimberly's coffee mug, and Louie brought out the carton of orange juice. The basset hound held it up to Kimberly, but she declined it with a nod. Elijah knew Kimberly wanted the orange juice, but she just wanted to be difficult toward Louie.

"Anything fun in *THEM Weekly*?" Kimberly asked as she picked up a strip of bacon and took a bite.

"Always." Elijah happily shared the details from the gossip magazine, which fed into their own family's gossip and their plans for the day.

"If the weather holds up, would you like to go for a walk by the pond with me?" Kimberly asked.

"See if we can find Shelly?" Elijah smiled with nostalgia.

They had been tracking an old, yellow-and-brown wood turtle that sat on logs throughout the summer.

"Oh, I hope so."

While they discussed their plans for the day, Ellie didn't say a word.

She didn't eat, Elijah thought as he hung his head low. As much as the heavy subject caused him discomfort, he had to let her come to them.

Ellie excused herself well before her parents had finished eating.

"Will you be joining us for meditation later?" Elijah asked Ellie.

"I'm going to meditate in my room." She stood from the table. "Come on, Louie."

They disappeared around the corner.

Following their usual breakfast and meditation, Elijah and Kimberly joined hands and walked from the house, through the woods and well-worn path, to the lovely, open pond a mile away. Frogs chirped, dragon flies zoomed around, and turtles stacked one on top of another.

"How is that old motorcycle coming along?" Kimberly asked.

"It's coming along." His chest tightened. He hated keeping secrets from her, but he had no choice. "I believe I'll be in need of a new project soon."

"Anything in mind?" She gently touched his forearm.

"A moat to keep your mother out."

Kimberly laughed and gently pushed him. "Seriously, anything calling to you?"

"Nah, not yet. I'm sure I'll find something."

On the floor of her bedroom, Ellie crossed her legs, and Louie took his usual spot at her side. With a heavy head, she sat tall, relaxed her shoulders, and let out a slow, mindful exhale as she closed her eyes. Ellie focused on her breath—the way it filled her lungs, expanded her diaphragm, and permeated her soul with a calming, soothing sensation. Her exhale slowly relaxed her body.

A creature of darkness.

She had to let it go. Her father's voice, though not present, played in her mind as she called forth his guidance.

"Let it slowly drift away."

Another slow, deep breath in.

Suddenly, she pictured a creature of no solid form—just a dark, thick ooze. It cascaded down in slow, viscous clumps, but as it turned to her, she saw a mouth—open as if to swallow her.

Something smacked her leg. Ellie jumped and opened her eyes.

"Hey, you're not breathing slowly." Louie's paw rested on her thigh. "Focus."

"I'm trying!" Ellie shook out her arms and rolled her head slowly from left to right. With her hands resting in her lap and a pinky on his paw, she tried again.

As soon as she closed her eyes, the creature was back. With an irritated sigh, she dropped her head.

Ellie-Lynne Betty Becker will meet her fate one spring eve.

Those once-hollow words hit her in the stomach like a mallet. Ellie's shoulders slumped forward, and her body trembled at the haunting prophecy.

"Ellie, what's wrong?" Louie broke his pose and climbed into her lap to face her.

Tears welled in her exhausted, bloodshot eyes, and she felt a wet nose pressed against her face. Ellie hugged Louie tight. "I'm scared, Louie," she admitted.

"Of what?" He huffed protectively. "Who's scaring you? Who do I have to beat up?"

"I'm scared.... I'm angry." Tears streamed down her face. "I'm hurt... why did they keep this from me?"

When she had control over her breathing and the sobs stopped, a wet nose met her nose. "What happened?"

Ellie shared her adventure in the library and her discovery of Betty Fischer's journal.

"Maybe she's wrong, though," Ellie said. "Everyone in the family described her as 'a bit off' because she was always humming, dancing, and talking to herself."

"Singing and humming? Sounds delightful," Louie added with a cheerful tone.

"Delightful?" A treacherous chuckle left her lips.

"Yeah, better than someone who is grumpy all the time." Louie continued, "Ellie, listen. You're letting your mother's interpretation of a clairvoyant's vision drive you to tears—"

"It says—"

"Please, don't interrupt." He pressed politely. "If you have a question about a car, who do you go see?"

"A mechanic."

"If you want the best bread of your life, who do you go see?"

"A baker."

"So, if you want an interpretation of a magical being's vision, where do you go?"

"A clairvoyant?"

"Well, y—"

A knock on the door interrupted them. "Ellie." It was her mother. "Can I come in?"

"I'm trying to meditate," Ellie called back, already annoyed by the sound of her mother's voice—the voice of secrets, treason, and deception.

"Sorry, it sounded like you were talking to that... to Louie. You didn't touch your breakfast. I wanted to see if you were feeling alright."

"Not really." It wasn't a lie, but Ellie wasn't exactly about to tell her the truth either. *I know about the prophecy, the suitors...*

"You should go back to bed when you're done, then. I can take care of the garden for you."

A day off? Ellie looked at Louie with raised eyebrows.

"Yeah, I think I'll take you up on that." Ellie tried not to sound too excited.

Eager to catch up on her sleep, she climbed back into bed. *Meditating can wait until later.*

"As I was saying, you don't go to a nervous-nelly bookworm with an active imagination to interpret visions." Louie plopped down on top of Ellie. He was like a comforting, toasty blanket. Nose to chin, paws on her shoulders, he nuzzled in. Softly, sweetly, Louie hummed the Seer's tune to her as she drifted off to sleep.

Ellie didn't dream of dripping, drooping, melting ghouls—or of pain and suffering. Instead, she had glorious dreams of dancing on the wind with the grace of a butterfly. She scaled glorious, tall peaks and touched the crests of breaking waves in warm oceans.

10

Freight Liner

O nline college?" Ellie raised her eyebrow. "That's your..."
Ellie shook her head and put her head into her hand. *She doesn't know that I know.*

"You could take a couple of prerequisites, get a feel for class structure before you really commit to it, you know?" Kimberly responded, desperately making her case. "You could really ease into it and take things at your own pace. So many kids are doing it these days, and you wouldn't have to worry about dorm life and what you would do with Louie."

Ellie sucked through her teeth as she tried to restrain herself. "College is the least of my concerns right now, Mom."

"You want more independence, right?" Kimberly kept going. "You could get a part-time job at the gas station, like you've been asking. Nothing too much, but maybe like ten hours a week so you could continue your potion-making with your dad."

"Mom, I've been through that book, like, a jillion times." Ellie's forehead was taught with irritation. "Why even—"

"You've been through the Becker book, not the Wagner book." Kimberly's eyebrows raised excitedly. "You could learn the—"

"What?" Ellie raised a hand in hopes her mother would stop talking. "There's another book?"

"Oh yes! Each family has their own unique takes on potions, and they even have completely different ones—"

"I've been studying potions for five years. Why didn't anybody ever tell me?" Ellie looked over to Louie, who shrugged.

"Well, honey, it was because your father only knows his family recipes, right? I can't teach you ours, so we'd need to set up a time with someone who can—maybe your cousin Megan."

Ellie's lips tightened as her frustrations boiled to the top.

"Or Lianne," her mother quickly corrected herself.

"Why wasn't this brought up years ago?" Ellie finally started to snap.

"We didn't want to rush—"

"That's crap! That's such bull crap."

"Excuse me?" Kimberly put her hand over her heart, a classic-Mee-Maw move.

"What would you know? Why was this your call? You have no idea what you're talking about! You don't know what it's like—"

"Because I'm your mother! Your teacher! I know what's best—"

"Best," Ellie snapped. "Best? Oh, that's rich!"

Anger boiled deep within her and seeped out to Ellie's fingers and toes. It was like electricity tingling each of her digits. Loose hairs on her stood as static ran through her. "Just like how you want to side with Mee-Maw on who should get to marry me?"

Kimberly's eyes widened.

"That's right. What was his name? Chris? Clark?"

"Kevin," Louie added.

"Thank you, Louie!" Ellie pointed down to him. "And by the way, is it so hard to be fricken nice to my Familiar? What has he ever done to you besides fetch you wine, wait on you hand and foot, and be respectful?"

The garage door opened, and Elijah came in. Ellie didn't break eye contact with her mother, though.

"Wha—" Kimberly started.

"Don't try to act all innocent! I'm not an idiot. I know *you*. I know how you are. You control everything! I can't attend a public school!" Ellie listed each item on her fingers. "I can't get a job! I can't use my driver's license! College, marriage, what next? You're going to tell me when I can have kids, too? Sorry, that doesn't fall on Kimberly's schedule. Her outline of events for—"

"Woah." Elijah stepped between them with grease-covered hands in the air. "Talking is respectful; name-calling and shouting isn't."

"And you let all of this happen!" Ellie pointed directly at her father.

He looked completely unprepared for the accusation.

"Are you ready to talk now, Dad? Let's talk about the arranged marriage. I reject them all! *All* of them! You know what I'm going to do?" She paced. "I'm going to live in the woods with Louie, grow my own food, and never be found by any of you ever again! How does that sound? You want to control everything? How about you get nothing! None of me."

"Ellie, please don't talk that way," Kimberly pleaded. "We don't have any choi—"

"Oh, and let's not forget. My time is limited, right? 'One spring eve, she will meet her fate!'"

Kimberly gasped loudly. Ellie looked at her father. He was as white as a ghost.

He knew about that, too. Her greatest human confidant. The person she trusted and looked up to for every major life decision. Her heart sank deep into her chest.

"You knew..." It was like a freight liner that sank into the depths of the ocean. "And you never told me... you let-. How could you?" Ellie's anger crumbled like an unstable Jenga tower.

"Everything I've done—" Elijah started to explain, but Ellie shook her head as her bottom lip protruded and trembled.

Heartbreak pushed anger from her and filled every inch of her body. *Run, run, run.*

At full speed, she hurried from the living room through the back door, down the main rows in the garden, and into the woods. With the sun low in the sky, the forest quickly grew dark. She had no idea where her feet would take her or what state they would be in when she got there. All she knew was she couldn't stay in that house a second longer.

Ellie passed rows and rows of apple trees and a large machine that rumbled over the ground as it cut grass between lanes. Soon, she was on the other side of the apple orchard, over the old, paved country road, and into thick brush on the other side. The old, wide, slow-moving river stopped her.

Now that Ellie was still, she felt her trembling legs collapse underneath her. Tears poured down her cheeks with each ragged breath.

"I'm here," Louie assured her as his nose met hers. "I've got you."

"Why!" she squeaked when she finally could get enough control to force air through her vocal cords. "Why would he—why wouldn't he tell me? Why would he keep all this from me? He knew everything! Everything, Louie."

Louie sat back to give Ellie more space to breathe. His eyes shimmered with concern.

"He was as bad as her, pulling the strings on my life."

"He's human, Ellie." A needy paw lifted towards her. "You all keep secrets."

"I don't care! It's not fair! It's my life! Me! Why am I the last to know everything?" She tore grass from the ground and threw it into the air around her. "Marriage! My death! Everything! What secrets do I get to have? When do I get to make my own choices?"

Ellie's body shivered as the last bits of rage dissipated, and she collapsed to the ground.

"I matter," she muttered through pouted lips. "I-I can't live someplace where I don't have control over my own life." Her voice was hoarse from screaming.

"Oh, Ellie." Louie rested his head against hers. "I know it hurts. It's okay to be angry. Sometimes, those who love us the most will disappoint us."

Ellie sighed and shook her head. "This is more than disappointment. This is... a-a betrayal... I can't trust them."

Thoughtfully, Louie looked up to the sky. He shifted his weight from side to side. "Trust is such a precious and fragile thing... it should be protected."

"Yes!" Ellie's shoulders relaxed as a tiny wave of relief washed over her.

"I can't begin to understand their reasoning for keeping things from you. I could understand if you were a child and they wanted to protect you from everything... I mean maybe they were trying to hold onto that a bit longer? I don't know."

Ellie took a deep breath to respond, but Louie continued.

"It doesn't make it right. Even birds know when to push the chicks out of the nest."

Ellie sighed wearily and lay down on her back. Above, the stars twinkled against the clear night sky. As her aching muscles slowly unclenched, the chorus of crickets and cicadas accompanied them. Louie laid his head against her stomach.

Soothed by the sounds of nature, the crisp air, and the stars sparkling above, Ellie felt her heart beat slow and her mind slowly open.

Why wouldn't they talk to me about the arranged marriages? It's not like it was completely unheard of. Mee-Maw kept bringing it up. Ellie rolled her eyes at the thought of her grandmother. The last time she saw her, the old bat tried to strike Ellie with her cane.

"They had so many opportunities to right it," she muttered to Louie. He shifted the weight of his head on her stomach. "Why arranged, though? Like, why can't I just find someone on my own? It doesn't make any sense."

"Tradition?" Louie tilted his head to the side.

Ellie raised her hand in confusion. "But whose tradition? Nobody on television goes through this unless they're from another country or because of some religion or something." Ellie scoffed, and her hand found his silky ear.

"Television isn't real life, Ellie." Louie took his chances and snuck further up her core. "People don't go around streets singing and dancing."

"You sure? I'd do it." A small smirk pulled at her lips.

"Oh, look who smiled." Louie lifted himself up and climbed onto her chest so he stood over her.

"Don't even think about—"

A big, wet tongue slipped up the middle of her face.

"Ugh! You jerk."

"She's so pretty! Look who's smiling." Louie continued his loving assault until she smiled wide, and laughter filled the air.

Ellie wrapped her arms around the fat dog and held him tightly to her chest. His nose nuzzled her chin. The moment her laughter stopped, the heartbreak crept back in.

Oh no. She swallowed hard. *This isn't going away.* Her smile faltered. "I think we have to go."

"Back home?"

"No." Her hand rubbed the back of his head. "Away from here. Some place big."

The Void calls.

Ellie couldn't bring herself to address that tonight. With a hopeful tone, she asked Louie, "Tell me our story again?"

As they lay there beneath the night sky, Louie told her their story once again. He told it the way she knew it, *her* version—not the rushed one he gave to her father. "Like the snap of fingers, suddenly, I was. I existed..."

Following the story, they made it back to the house after midnight. Nobody was up to greet them.

Thank the Void.

"Go lay down. I will get the salve," Louie instructed as he headed into the pantry.

Walking on the outsides of her feet, Ellie made her way back to her bedroom. She sat back on her bed and pulled her filthy feet up to look at them. There were cuts, pebbles, and a couple of thorns in the bottom of them.

When Louie arrived, he had the breadbasket in his mouth, which contained a deep dish of water, a clean washcloth, and the salve.

"What's all of that?" Ellie asked from the edge of her bed.

"Well, I figured your feet are probably dirty, too." He nudged the washcloth with his nose. "Want me to clean them for you?"

"No." She chuckled. "I can do this myself. Why don't you start packing our things?"

"What?" he asked. "Now? We're really going to leave?"

She nodded. "Yeah, now. I can't stay here anymore, Louie. I have to get away."

"Where will we go?"

"I don't know yet, but anywhere is better than here."

After cleaning her feet, Ellie lathered them with the off-white paste. The smell of mint hung in the air until her skin absorbed all of it. As Ellie sat on her bed with her feet up, she watched Louie gather the items they discussed, including Betty Fischer's journal, for their trip.

She heard her wooden desk chair screech against the wooden floorboards, and when she looked up, she saw Louie climb up onto the chair and then onto her desk. He stretched out his oblong body and popped the thumbtacks off her map of the United States. Not only did he gather the map in a careful manner, but he managed to push the thumbtacks back into the corkboard, so they didn't step on any loose ones.

"Bud, you amaze me."

Louie beamed and stumbled on his long ear as he hopped off the desk.

The alarm clock displayed 3:05a.m. Ellie stood at the side of her bed. Her old hiking backpack was empty, and all the contents she was about to shove into it lay on the bed.

Extra socks, food, fresh water... that should get us to the next town.

Louie had placed their old camping and hiking gear across the bed. Tied together with a hair tie, she had a tight wad of money she had hoarded over the years from holidays, birthdays, and odd jobs she did for the family. And lastly, she had Ahren's journal and her biography.

"Ebeeben," Louie announced as he hopped up with her white-and-orange-tipped EpiPen in his mouth. It was like the pen glared back at her, mocking her in Kimmy's voice.

"Thank you," she said flatly. "So what about Boston—to start out?"

"Wherever, you want to go is okay with me," Louie replied. "As long as we're together, I'm happy."

Ellie smiled. "Okay, so if we take the Trunkline Trail, we should be in Boston in about three days, assuming we do about twenty miles per day."

"Slow poke," Louie teased.

"You're one to talk. What's the clearance you have on that thing?" She pointed to his tummy. "Four inches?"

"Kept up with you when you were running," he reminded her smugly.

They reviewed the mental packing list for the fourth time before they finally packed the gray and purple backpack. Ellie shoved the money in her pocket. They had just over five hundred dollars.

Should be enough. With her knowledge of forageable herbs and that money, they could probably make it until she landed a job. *Louie doesn't need to eat anything.*

When she stood after lacing her hiking boots, a flutter of excitement ran through her body. It was well past 3 a.m. at this point, so the threat of running into her parents was non-existent.

"Ready, buddy?"

"Ready!" Louie hopped into her arms so his nails didn't click against the floorboards—a detail they didn't overlook.

The hallway outside her room never looked so long, dark, or unnerving. With each step, it was like her shoes were just a smidgen too loud, too heavy, or just not in the right spot. It took them three times longer than normal to pass the library, her parents' bedroom, and to the front door. Ellie reached out to grab the doorknob when Louie stopped her.

"Wait! The hinges. Take the garage door."

"Right! Good idea," she whispered and turned around. Ellie doubled back and took them to the garage door, just across from the living room. To her dismay, the garage was fully lit. The car was up on the oil change ramp, and music softly played. Elijah stood there, oil smeared on his cheek and his hair held back by a bandanna and a ponytail.

11

Goggles

eading out?" Elijah wiped his hands on the old red rag. The smell of motor oil lingered in the air, even with the garage door open.

"Yeah." She couldn't look him in the eye.

Elijah beckoned them into the garage and gestured for Ellie to shut the door behind her. Once it was shut, he spoke. "I knew this day would come."

He didn't smile. She studied him quizzically as she held Louie and cautiously stepped into the garage. *Does he have a swat team ready to bag me up on the other side of the garage door? What would they even do with me? It's not like there's a jail on Azalea Way... but there is a basement full of spider webs.*

In his stoic way, Elijah walked over to his work bench, tossed the well-loved red rag onto the bench, and turned his attention to the wall near the steel storage cabinet. Ellie didn't need to see the words on the wall to know they were there.

EB&EB Garage-where anything can happen!

Ellie kept herself just out of arms reach in case he turned on her. He never laid a hand on her before or gave any indication that he had a propensity for violence, but Ellie wasn't sure she could trust him anymore.

"Now, where did I..." Elijah mumbled as he opened one cabinet drawer after another. Nuts, bolts, and other handy-man accouterments shifted and smacked against the steel drawers. "There we go."

Pleased, Elijah pulled a standard white envelope covered in black grease and scratch marks out of the depths of one of the drawers. It was thick.

"Before I give this to you, promise me you won't be stupid."

Ellie raised an eyebrow.

"You won't be proud," he corrected himself. "Before you go hungry, before you do inexplicable things to make money..." Elijah's eyes winced at the thought of it. "Call."

He has such a way with words. Ellie chuckled with relief and shook her head. "Yeah, promise." *Not that he deserves a promise.*

Elijah gestured for her to turn around. Ellie lifted her head suspiciously.

"I was going to put it in your backpack, honey," Elijah informed her.

Ellie looked down at Louie, and he gave her a quick nod. She set him down on the ground and directed her back toward her father. The hiking backpack's clips clicked, the zipper zipped, and Ellie stumbled back on her heels as he made room for the envelope in the full backpack.

"You have your water bottle with the filter?" Elijah asked as he closed the backpack.

"Yes."

"Thermal blanket?"

"Yes."

"Money?"

"Some." Ellie reminded herself to keep the depths of her preparation to herself. *He could still turn.*

"I know you may not be in the mood to talk to me right now." Before she could reply, he added, "Completely justified."

Ellie's head and shoulders slumped; she hated that he took the wind out of her sails.

"I just—I love you, sweetheart. More than you can ever know." Elijah clasped his hands. "I understand the fear your mother has, but you're a grown woman. You need the space and the ability to make your own choices, your own mistakes, and your own memories."

This was everything Ellie had wanted to hear for years. The tension in her body relaxed, even though a part of her wanted to make him suffer more for his betrayal.

Elijah gestured over to the far side of the garage. They walked together as he spoke. "There are two things I know to be certain..."

An old, paint-splattered tarp covered a large object in the corner by the doorway. He removed the bricks and rocks he used to keep the tarp over the "Classified" object.

"You can't stop fate, and you, Ellie, are just too big for Azalea Way."

Elijah pulled back the tarp to reveal a 1979 Honda CB650, an older motorcycle that didn't have the fuss and frills of newer models. The last time Ellie saw this bike, she was sixteen, and it looked like there was no hope for it. Back then, it was composed of rusted pipes and a torn leather seat. Now, it looked completely new.

Chrome pipes and mechanical bits sat toward the front of the bike, and the thick muffler shimmered like dew on a blade of grass in the morning sun. The gas tank and covered areas were no longer the rusted, chipped, deep blue she had originally seen. Elijah had painted them a deep purple that shimmered when the light hit it. The forks and wheel spokes were painted in a lime green accent. The once-torn double seat was now brand-new leather. He even added a windshield to the front of the bike.

What made this bike extra wonderful and extra special, in Ellie's opinion, was the sidecar. It was probably nothing exceptional when he first bought it, just a boxy design with a wide seat and big wheels, but Elijah painted it to match the motorcycle. On the inside of the bike, she saw words in her father's handwriting:

EB & EB Garage—where anything can happen! Be safe.

Tears infiltrated Ellie's eyes.

"There's a step," Louie exclaimed and hopped on the small, plastic step between the outer wheel and the body of the sidecar. Louie slipped out of sight inside the sidecar, then back out as he explored his new space. "This is great!"

"I'm glad you like it, but that's not all." Elijah reached into the depths of the leg space and pulled out a plastic sheet. "I figured Louie might enjoy the wind in his face, but I have this, in case he wants to be covered. This Velcros into place and unzips. He can keep an eye on you and not get bugs in his cheeks."

"Oh, there's more." Louie disappeared and reappeared with a leather jacket, a helmet, and gloves for Ellie, as well as a miniature helmet and goggles.

"Those are for you." Elijah took the goggles and helped secure them to Louie's head. They strapped securely under his ears. A secondary strap went under his chin. "Polarized, so the glare shouldn't blind you."

"Someone's looking fly." Ellie patted Louie on his head. The basset hound sat with his haunches off to the side and his paws situated in front of him, so his chest dutifully puffed out. *I could smother him in kisses right now.*

Elijah grabbed the jacket and held it up for Ellie to put on. It was a bit of a process as she took off her backpack, her jacket, and her long-sleeved sweater, revealing her comfortable T-shirt.

"Every time you ride, please wear this jacket and that helmet." He helped her pull it over her shoulders.

She turned around. Just like when she was six, and the winter gloves were too bulky for her to zip her own jacket, Elijah grabbed the zipper and pulled it up.

A perfect fit.

"I don't care what state law says or how hot it is. Being sweaty is a small price to pay to protect the skin on your arms or face."

"I understand." As much as she wanted to hold on to her anger, it was hard to do now. *He planned this better than I did.* "Dad?"

"Yeah?"

"How did you know?"

"How did I know what?" Elijah gathered up the gloves for her.

"That we'd leave?"

"You're my daughter." Elijah handed her the gloves. "Don't need Betty Fischer to know every bird needs to leave the nest."

Louie took it upon himself to pack the leg space with their belongings.

"You picked one hell of a night to go. Supposed to be clear skies... walk the bike to the end of the road, then start it up, or Mee-Maw will blow your cover."

He's thought of everything.

"I have one last thing to ask of you." Ellie listened humbly. "One last midnight snack? Cookies and milk?" Elijah's expression softened, and he gently kicked a loose rock on the floor and tucked his hands into his pockets. "I understand if you say no, but I just can't have you leave with things like this between us."

The radio played softly behind them as the stars twinkled above. Ellie, Louie, and Elijah sat on the floor of the garage, their legs crossed, with a container of store-bought cookies in front of them. A shooting star rushed across the sky.

"I know you're hurt, and an apology won't magically fix this or heal the damage that has been done," Elijah began. "I just hope one day you can understand that I've done everything to protect you. All of this—the prophecy, Oren breathing down our necks, the arranged marriages—they all kept me awake so many nights. Every choice I considered, every possibility, they ended terribly."

He's right; an apology won't 'fix' this. It won't change what was said or done.

"And being married... I just... when you're married, you can't make decisions on your own. You have to make them together. Being a parent is the most wonderful thing—and the hardest thing," Elijah added.

"What's the hardest thing about it?" Ellie pressed.

Elijah ran his hand through his hair, tugged out his ponytail, and secured it all over again. "That's a tough one..." He passed her another cookie. "Maybe navigating how to let go? I remember the first time you told us you 'hated' us. I knew it was just the frustrations and lack of understanding of a child, but..." Elijah exhaled sharply. "It stung."

Ellie half-heartedly chuckled.

"I know you're an adult. Honestly, you've been an adult for a little while now. I just... I hope one day you can forgive me for everything."

Ellie couldn't help but notice how he never bit into his next cookie. She took the cookie he had passed to her and split it with Louie, who still wore his helmet and goggles.

"For what it's worth, I think you did alright." Ellie's tone was flat, but she couldn't keep herself from smiling. "You know, the parenting thing."

When Elijah saw the smile she was trying to hide, he gave her a playful shove.

"Gonna have a hell of a morning in front of you," Ellie said as she shoved the rest of the cookie in her mouth.

"Yup." Elijah sounded like he desperately dreaded it. "And the part of me that can be your friend, that's the one who's taking this blow for you."

"The one that fixed up that bike?" Ellie asked with a smirk.

"No. That's the dad-side. Can't let the bird out of the nest without some means of transportation, right?"

Ellie shrugged. "Can I ask you about the suitors?"

"Of course."

"Do I know them?"

"You met them all... remember your Becoming Ceremony?"

Ellie's eyebrows pulled together tight, and she shook her head from side to side. "All I remember is this guy." She pointed at the basset hound beside her.

"Well, maybe that's a good thing." Elijah smiled with eyes that looked haunted by the memory. Elijah looked down at the pavement and picked away at a loose piece of rubble formed by a crack.

I hate seeing him like this.

Finally, he broke the silence. "Don't worry. None of them were your type."

Ellie brayed with laughter.

When the cookies were gone, Elijah passed the keys to Ellie. The key-chain was endearingly decorated with a cursive "E" and "L" intertwined.

"Ellie and Louie?" she asked as she inspected it.

Elijah nodded.

Louie found his way back into the sidecar and assumed his seat, goggles at the ready. Elijah walked Ellie and the bike down the driveway before he dug into his pocket. He pulled out a small, flip cell phone.

"Call. Once a week?"

"I promise." Ellie passed it off to Louie, who found it a home amongst their things.

"And don't you ever feel too proud to call for help. You're lost. You're hurt. You need money—if I find out you didn't call, I will never forgive you!"

Ellie nodded.

"And if anyone approaches you from Oren, in long sleeve shirts or windbreakers, with short-cut hair, you don't speak to them, and you run." Elijah stared at Ellie.

"I don't get the Oren stuff," she said.

"I know. That's a story for another day. Just promise me," Elijah said.

"Okay," she replied awkwardly.

"I'm serious, Ellie," he said more sternly.

"Okay, weirdo, okay." She held her hands up in defeat. "I won't talk to anyone from Oren."

"Thank you." Elijah's shoulders relaxed, and he looked at the bike with sadness in his eyes.

Ellie couldn't remain angry with her father after all of this. She put out her arms, and he eagerly pulled her in for a tight embrace. "I love you, Dad."

"I love you too." He held on to her longer than he normally would. When he released her, he gently nodded towards the road. "Now, go on."

Ellie grabbed the handle bars and strained to push the heavy machine to get some momentum.

"Protect my little girl," Elijah requested of Louie as the bike rolled away.

Louie nodded to Elijah.

With a crank of the handlebars to the right, they rolled out onto the road. Ellie looked back over her shoulder as they walked down the dark road. The light from the garage and the silhouette of her father just over the driveway hedges remained until they were completely out of sight. The sun threatened to break the skyline as they hit the end of Azalea Way, out of reach of Beckers and Wagners. Then, Ellie started her new motorcycle.

Thanks, Dad. Ellie remembered the day he taught her how to ride one of these.

"Turn the key," Elijah had instructed her. "Turn on the petcock and open the choke."

She followed his instructions, and the engine roared to life. She secured her helmet to her head. Then, with a twist of the right handle and a turn of the handlebars, they were off of Azalea Way, down the road toward the interstate.

12

Boston

*T*ake *I-395 to Auburn, then I-90 East to Boston,* Elijah had told Ellie over cookies. *Avoid rush hour traffic between 7 a.m. and 9 a.m., 3 p.m. and 6 p.m. It will be too scary and overwhelming for you.*

For the first half an hour, the drive up I-395 was peaceful. At 4 a.m., nobody was on the road except for a few eighteen-wheelers. *Those things are massive.* Their size and might made Ellie's chest tighten as she zipped past them.

Ellie tried to shout over the whipping of the wind. "I don't like those trucks, Louie!"

Unable to take her eyes off the road, with white knuckles on the handlebars, they pushed on. It wasn't until they hit the sign for Weston that the scenery changed. Overhead bridges and massive green signs demanded her attention with reflective paint, and the road gained an extra lane. Beautiful trees gave way to cold-looking storefronts, dilapidated apartment buildings, and train tracks covered in graffiti. At Alston, there were no more trees, a fourth lane, and more cars.

"Keep a cool head," Louie called out to her. "If it gets to be too much, just slow down and take an exit. We can figure it out."

Except Ellie only heard the wind as it rushed past. Out of the corner of her eyes, she saw his lips flapping like curtains in a rainstorm.

As the sun peeked over the horizon, black gave way to shades of purple and, eventually, pink. The closer she got to Boston, the less cold and desolate the buildings felt. The bridges over the interstate now had chain-link fences along the sides. Some bridges had signs draped along them.

Never give up

The encouraging words brought a smile to Ellie's face.

Emerson for School Board

That one looked out of place to her.

Soon, the city skyline came into view. By five, cars were out and about, so the streets were congested.

Oh no. Ellie swallowed hard as she became boxed in around other drivers. *They're really close.*

Buildings became large and soulless. Ellie's breath caught in her chest. An uneasy, crushing feeling overcame her as they drove beneath a massive dark building into a prolonged bridge—or so she thought. Trapped inside a cement box, surrounded by other drivers who demanded she speed around the tight corners, Ellie's shoulders tightened, and she squeezed the handlebars. Hideous yellowed lights buried along the concrete walls created an eerie glow. It felt hot. Other drivers swerved into her lane, honking and screaming at her.

"Louie," she cried out as she was forced to follow the flow to the right.

Prudential Square
Exit Only

If she dared push back to the left, she would risk running headfirst into a sharp cement wall dividing the lanes. Traffic forced them into a harsh, continuous turn to the right that made Louie slide across his seat and slam into the side of the car.

"Hold on tight," she screamed as the motorcycle and sidecar screeched around the corner. Ellie held onto the handlebars with all her might, her face distorted with concentration. It was like a splash of cold water in her face as the darkness dropped away, and they were met by beams of early morning sunlight.

The road didn't lead to open spaces, though. Instead, she saw large parking garages, shimmering glass buildings, and more unwelcoming concrete. People populated the brick sidewalks. Her thighs gripping the motorcycle seat, Ellie kept the bike straight and followed the flow of traffic. Light after light, her heart rate slowed, and adrenaline melted away.

"You did such a good job," Louie said as he perched on the sidecar.

"Thank you," Ellie muttered as she became aware of how damp her armpits and forehead felt.

HONK!

She jumped in her seat, and her heart raced again.

HONK!

"Stop it," Ellie shouted. Louie turned his attention to the other car and put on a convincing show in his role of a basset hound.

The car beside her bullied her into the left turn as the current of cars pushed through the green light. The driver shouted at her through a cracked window.

"I don't want to go into another tunnel, Louie!" Tears welled in her eyes.

"I don't see a tunnel! Just pull over!"

Ellie tried to find a break in the traffic, an open parking spot—anything.

Just beyond the tops of cars, bright, green, bushy trees popped up into her view. Birds flew away and off into the sky above.

"Go!" She willed herself forward.

As she pulled up, a car signaled to pull out of a parking space along the busy street. *Oh, thank the Void!* Ellie stopped and allowed them to cut in. As soon as she was parked, she cut the engine, pulled her helmet from her head, and shook out her hair.

"We made it," she exclaimed as the cool, refreshing air ran through her damp hair.

"Help," Louie called out. Ellie looked into the side car and found Louie struggling to pull off his helmet and goggles. His back legs folded over on himself, and his paws dug into the rim of the goggles.

"Oh, stop." Ellie laughed and poked his vulnerable backside.

"Hey!" He kicked at her hand with one of his fat paws.

She set her helmet down on top of the sidecar, stepped off the motorcycle, and knelt beside him. With the tug of a simple nylon strap, the helmet loosened, and she pulled it off his head. The goggles came with it. "Better?"

"That was exhilarating," Louie exclaimed and pulled himself upright.

"What are you talking about? That was terrifying! You saw how close those cars got. We were almost roadkill. People are crazy drivers here."

Louie snorted and hopped out of the sidecar, climbed down the hood, and landed with a thump on the sidewalk.

Ellie tucked their helmets inside the sidecar and pulled out the hiking backpack. As she tugged the heavy bag, she noticed how sore her arms were from being tense for so long. She let out a grunt as she tossed it over her shoulder and secured the support straps around her chest.

"Why don't we get some ice cream?" he asked with big, sweet eyes. "To celebrate how good of a job you did driving."

"Not right now, buddy." Ellie didn't know how he had an appetite after all that stress. "Boston's big, and I don't know where we are. Let's explore this park and see if we can find some place away from all these cars."

Ellie had only been to a park on a playground with swings, bullies, and slides. This park had paved walkways, litter, and overly manicured trees that seemed thoughtfully placed. It was beautiful—but not beautiful like a forest. Lamp posts made of black metal with large, bulbous lights on top of them sprinkled the tree line. Benches already had visitors—some of whom she assumed spent the night there by their posture across the flat wood.

"Let's have a seat under that tree." Ellie pointed to a large oak away from the path. Cigarette butts decorated the grass around its bare base. It looked like a frequently visited spot. *Uck.* Ellie looked around at the other trees, but this somehow still seemed like the most appealing option. "Let's make the best of it."

After removing the cigarette butts from their smelling radius, she sat with her back against the tree. Before her, she saw the imposing skyline of the city. As much as it should have intimidated her, it brought a smile to Ellie's face.

We made it.

"Should we meditate?" Louie broke the silence and looked awkwardly up at her. His silly head was upside down as they made eye contact. Those long ears dangled down toward her lap. "Ease those nerves?"

"Sure."

Ellie tied the strap of the backpack to her foot and the other strap to the bottom opening of the helmet. Unlike all the other times before, Louie did not climb off her lap. He waited patiently for her.

"Ready?"

"Yeah." Ellie closed her eyes, lengthened her spine, and relaxed her shoulders, letting out a slow, mindful exhale. Once again, she focused on her breath as it filled her lungs. She expanded her diaphragm and filled her soul with a calming, soothing sensation. With each breath, her body relaxed.

***

It wasn't long before the hustle and bustle of morning traffic stirred Ellie from sleep. The sound of honking horns echoed between the buildings. She opened her eyes, and the harsh, bright light of a beautiful day greeted her.

I could sleep for so many more hours.

The world had an odd sort of tint to it, like a light-blue haze of sorts. When she looked down at Louie, his eyes were locked onto her with a gentle, light-blue glow.

"Woah!" She jumped back, startled. The moment she did, the light faded, and Louie jumped on her lap, confused.

"Did you sleep well, Ellie?" he asked sweetly.

"Alright, you?"

"Oh, I didn't sleep. Gotta keep you safe." Louie puffed out his chest.

"Is that what you were doing? With those creepy demon eyes?"

"They were creepy?" Louie's voice grew small. "They never... well—it's not the first time I've done that."

"Oh yeah?" She scoffed. "Please, go on."

"I didn't mean to creep you out." His sad, elongated puppy eyes tugged at her heart.

Ellie couldn't resist the urge to comfort him with a pet.

"It's an aura of protection," Louie explained. "It's not super powerful, but it keeps the ants from biting you and makes people think twice about hanging out here."

I'm such a jerk. Ellie looked down towards the ground. Thousands of ants crawled around in the bare bits of grass, and she cringed. "Ew!" Quickly, she retreated and brushed her hands over her pants. "Ew, ew, ew, ew!" Ellie hopped from one foot to the other as she tried to shake away the feeling of tiny legs tickling her skin. Her backpack awkwardly held her leg down.

"You're fine," Louie reassured her. "I kept them all away."

Ellie shuddered. "Yick! Can still feel it, though."

She shook out her hair before she untied the backpack around her ankle. After a quick inspection, every zipper and item that hung from it looked like it was how it should be.

"Ten years," a woman shrieked at the top of her lungs. Ellie's head snapped toward the path they came from. "I gave him ten years of my life!"

The woman with brown hair was dressed in a loose-fitting, dirty tank top that looked like it would slip off her sickly frame. She stopped screaming for a moment and concentrated on the cigarette between her lips she wanted to light. A plastic bottle of some beverage dangled weakly from her free hand.

"Poor woman. She sounds like she's in so much pain," Ellie whispered to Louie. "Should we help her?"

"I don't think there's any helping her." He placed a thoughtful paw on top of her shoe. "Stay here."

"Ten years, and he just fu—" she cursed and punched the side of an aluminum trash can. The sound echoed in the tight space, through the trees, and got lost within the noises of the city. It sent a shock through Ellie, and she became aware of her own heartbeat. The woman muttered and mumbled to herself as she stumbled off the path onto the grass towards them.

"Those were her cigarettes on the ground." Louie released Ellie. "Let's go."

"And you let it all happen!" The half-empty bottle sailed through the air and fell short of them.

With hurried footsteps, Ellie and Louie walked deeper into the park, following the cement paths that soon gave way to brick. Black iron gates lined the edge of the grass as they spotted a gazebo-like monument. The labyrinth was beautiful and the scenes unpredictable. At one point, they crossed a pond with a docking area and small boats shaped like swans. The sign said, 'Closed.'

"Bud, before we leave, we *have* to take a swan-boat ride," Ellie added softly as they walked past the pond.

"I'd love that."

As the sun rose higher in the sky, more patrons populated the park. Some were accompanied by dogs; others had instruments in hand and kept a case with coins in it at their side. Ellie's friendly smile was either met with overly friendly grins, men with uncomfortable comments, scowls, or looks of disgust.

"Chin up," Louie encouraged her as he trotted along at Ellie's side.

"Shh. Dogs don't talk, remember?" She kept her voice low.

"Right." Louie covered his words with a dramatic sneeze. Trees lined the walkway and beautifully hung over it. Louie held his head high as he walked past other dogs who approached him with excitement. When one went to sniff his butt, Louie kicked it in the face with his back leg. "Personal space."

"Did your dog just—"

"No." Ellie cut off the stranger before the conversation could continue.

As off-putting as the manufactured park initially was, the attention to detail and careful placement of benches, trashcans, and flowers grew on Ellie.

"Do you think the law doesn't apply to you?" A female voice broke Ellie's serene moment.

Curiously, she looked up and saw a young woman with blond hair pulled back into a ponytail. Beside her, a fluffy, yellow, and white short dog did its business against one of the trees.

"Me?" Ellie put her hand on her chest.

"Yeah! You! Where's your leash?" the woman snapped.

"Leash?" Ellie looked down at Louie, who returned her confused gaze.

"Yeah! All owners! All dogs! Leash up!" With a tug on the leash, the corgi stumbled forward and stood beside her owner's leg. "Probably doesn't have his shots, does he? Or neutered?"

Ellie reeled away from the woman. "C'mon, Louie."

"You're a terrible person. You know that?" she yelled as Ellie walked away. "You're lucky I don't report you."

Ellie's heart thumped in her chest. "Jeez, what's her problem?"

"Just keep walking," Louie muttered and kept close to her side.

As they walked, Ellie kept her head low. She didn't want to welcome any other unnecessary confrontation. Her cheeks felt warm, and she was oddly aware of the existence of her ears.

What's with everybody here? She wiped her hands against her pant legs. *Crazy, mean, loud, gross. It's like a rotten beehive filled with-with wasps or squirrel poop.*

They picked up their pace as they hurried out of the park toward the closest exit. The buildings grew taller, with busier traffic and more pedestrian congestion.

How can people live like this? So on top of each other.

Some buildings were modern with lots of reflective glass, while others were old, beautiful cement buildings with detailed sculpture work accenting the ridges. Colorful banners occasionally hung from the sides of the buildings, advertising different schools, shows, and products.

Clip, clop, clip, clop.

Ellie lifted her head in the direction of the familiar sound. Along the wide sidewalk, a tall, beautiful, brown horse with a white underbelly trotted toward them. Louie protectively stood in front of Ellie as the massive, muscular creature approached. The rider was a middle-aged man in a black police uniform. "Morning, miss," he called out as they drew near.

"Good morning, Officer." Ellie put on her friendliest smile. She, admittedly, had never spoken with a police officer before. His presence made her heart flutter in her chest. *Oh gods, what does he want?*

"Cute pup you have there. Where's its leash?"

Ellie's eyes grew wide, and she looked down at Louie for help. Those big, brown eyes looked back at her helplessly. "I, uh..."

"All dogs must be leashed in city limits."

"Sorry, we just got to town this morning. I-I will get it taken care of."

"He tagged?"

"Tagged?" Her voice cracked.

"Yeah, a dog license. If he isn't licensed to you, then someone can just run off with him. Where are you from?"

"Connecticut."

He grumbled something about tourists under his breath. "Passing through or not, the law still applies. Get a leash on him, and for your sake, get him tagged. I see him off leash again, you'll get a ticket."

A ticket? Ellie nodded and backed up toward the iron metal gate of the sidewalk. *We haven't even been away from home for eight hours, and I'm in trouble with the law.*

Heat overwhelmed her, and her back met the iron fence that encapsulated the park. Ellie pulled off her backpack and leather jacket as she tried to catch her breath. Her knees wobbled as she gained distance from the police officer. She grabbed the metal gate and braced herself as she lowered herself to the ground. The moment she was seated, Louie climbed onto her lap and extended his nose toward her.

"Focus on your breathing," he whispered.

"A ticket?" Her voice shook. "I-I can't. Why?"

"He said *if*," Louie spoke slowly and deliberately. "We have a rope in the backpack. Tie that to my collar. We will be okay. Now focus."

Ellie rested her forehead against his wet nose and tried to gain control of her breathing.

"In..." Louie led her through thoughtful, deep breaths. "And out."

When Ellie was calm, she lifted her head up just far enough so she could look into his gentle eyes. "I don't want to put you on a leash, buddy. It's like forcing you to sit on the floor during dinner."

"I'll be okay," he reassured her with a soft tone. "It'll keep us from getting in trouble, so put it on me, and let's get you some breakfast. You must be starving."

Ellie kissed the dog on top of his head before she pulled her back-pack up towards them. With his encouragement and his permission, Ellie tied one end of the rope loosely to his collar with a large bundle of excess rope in her hand. The image of Louie with a rope tied to him made her heart feel heavy. She hated seeing him like this, treated like an actual dog. It was beneath him.

Stupid jerks. He's a Familiar. He deserves to be treated with some respect.

All secured, under the letter of the law, Louie hopped off Ellie's lap and waited for her to repack the bag. When she stood, they walked down the street with their sights set on breakfast food.

13

The Cost of Living

The Bluffin' Muffin Cafe, a snug establishment that ran parallel to the north side of the park, was tucked into the first floor of a massive, modern glass building. A solid wooden sign with the cafe's name burnt into it hung above the beautiful, heavy wooden door. To the right of the entrance, a large glass window with white paint decorations that spiraled into one another welcomed guests. From the outside, it looked like a cafe she could find nestled somewhere in the woods of Connecticut, like something from a story book. The heavy, wooden front door swung gracefully on its hinges, and the chime of bells greeted Ellie. When she looked up, she didn't find any bells but a motion-activated little black speaker box.

Of course. Thanks, Boston.

Inside, the cafe didn't fit the vibe of the outside. It felt sterile and fake. Where Ellie expected to see bookshelves, board games, and comfy chairs, she saw small, perfectly square tables with plastic black-and-clear napkin holders. Many of the tables were covered in crumbs from previous patrons. The baristas looked like cookie-cutter people plucked out of a commercial. Each barista wore a brown hat with coffee-colored designs of the logo, matching deep brown aprons, cream-colored long-sleeve shirts rolled up to their elbows, and frowns that only broke for a moment when they said, "Welcome."

"Excuse me, miss," the cashier barked in a way that didn't match the politeness of her words. "No dogs allowed. You'll have to leave him outside."

The cashier's raised eyebrows made Ellie feel two inches tall. *How was I supposed to know?* Her heart dropped into her stomach as she turned to look at Louie's long face. His big brown eyes held hers as the realization of tying him up was imminent.

"I hate this," she whispered.

"Muffin?" He tried to disguise the word with a bark.

Ellie closed her eyes and let out a sigh. His terrible attempt to cover up the words made a chuckle rise in her chest, but the heaviness of her heart held it down like a cement brick. *He deserves better than this.*

"Yes, I'll get you a blueberry muffin... can you wait outside for me, please?"

Louie looked from side to side before he opened his mouth to catch his rope leash. Ellie watched through the door as he took the rope to the light post outside and walked it around to tie himself up.

Begrudgingly, she joined the small, slow-moving line. *Nothing's like I expected it to be. Sure, buildings, lots of people, even funky smells, but it all seems so fake and distant.* She glanced to the other end of the counter to a sign that read, Pick-Up.

The patrons wore headphones, avoided eye contact with each other, and looked down at their brick-like phones.

They're so disconnected from one another. Where's the polite smiles? The friendly chatter? The cement is more welcoming than the people.

"And for you, miss?" The barista she spoke with before stood behind the counter. The way she glared at Ellie only solidified how Ellie was feeling.

"Two blueberry muffins and two big vanilla lattes."

That's what they ask for in my shows. Ellie tried to put a positive spin on the situation. *I can finally try it.*

A smirk pulled at her lips as she thought of the lists of potions she knew. She could heal a cut, ease itchiness, and even suck out venom, but healing a broken heart? There was no herb for that.

"That'll be $33.27."

Ellie's eyes widened. *Two muffins and two cups of coffee, well, lattes, which were just a different form of a cup of coffee. How could that be thirty dollars?*

"Is that correct?" Ellie asked timidly.

"Two extra-large vanilla lattes, $9.99 each, and two large blueberry muffins, $5.56 each. After tax, that's $33.27."

"How much would it be with a regular-sized muffin?" Her cheeks felt warm.

"We only carry large." The cashier looked tired of the conversation. She blinked with such ferocity, Ellie expected the long eyelashes to fly off her sparkly blue eyelids.

The line behind her shifted and muttered with irritation. The tension crawled up Ellie's back like an excited squirrel up a tree. She didn't want to draw more attention, so she reluctantly pulled out two twenties from her pocket and handed them to the cashier.

When she received her change, that same little green monster that encouraged her to switch the coaster and notepad two nights ago in the library reared its ugly head. Ellie let her eyes linger on the tip jar, then looked up at the barista. With pursed lips, Ellie raised her eyebrows and let out a small "Hm" before she followed the signs to the side of the counter where other patrons stood waiting for their orders. Everyone stood in silence at the end of the counter. Her mind wandered to Deedee's Corner Store.

One of the places where I wanted to work.

There, she could pick up a large, fresh, home-made muffin for three dollars. A cup of coffee was a dollar.

"Two muffins and two vanilla lattes," a male barista with dark features called out as he set a paper bag on the counter and two paper cups with white plastic tops. Ellie stepped forward to grab it, but another patron snatched the order before she could make it up to the counter.

Wait, what happened? Was that mine? She sank back awkwardly.

The next patron had a bagel and an iced coffee. Then, a vanilla chai latte.

"Two muffins and two extra-large vanilla lattes."

There! Ellie sprung forward and snatched it before any other miscalculations could occur.

Through the fake chimes, Ellie emerged back onto the city sidewalk. Louie politely stood out of pedestrians' way, holding the rope-leash in his mouth. Nearly every person who walked by stopped, kneeled, and gave him a gentle pat on the head with an obligatory "Good boy" or "Good job."

His wide chest, which was perfectly white except for a tiny brown dot, puffed out with pride. His fat feet accumulated wrinkles from his legs, like ill-fitting tall socks. Louie's long brown ears hung well past his saggy neck, and he had puppy eyes that could negotiate the release of a full slice of pizza from a starving man.

He is the cutest thing on this planet.

He looked up to Ellie, his mouth agape with a question.

"Yes, I got you a muffin," she assured him before he could speak. "Let's find a place to sit."

They trotted back toward the park and found the closest available seat. Louie dropped his bundle of rope between them and patiently waited for his muffin.

"I got you a latte, too, so we could try it together," Ellie said as she set up their breakfast before them.

"Oh," he exclaimed and tried to cover it up as a little howl.

Ellie bit her lip to hide her chuckle. "Be careful, you goofball. It's really hot," she warned him.

"I'm made of hot," he whispered with pride as he peeled off the lid of his vanilla latte with his teeth. With a quick lap of his tongue, he looked like he was in heaven. "Mmm." The dog went back and forth between his muffin and latte, much like a human would.

With a large bite, Ellie's mouth was filled with dry, tasteless bits of muffin. *Did they mix it with sand, then freeze it? I can't believe I paid six bucks for this!* Disgusted, she set it down on the bench. The latte, though—oh, that was heavenly. Creamy, smooth, and a perfect hint of vanilla. *Not worth ten bucks, but I'll take it.*

"Excuse me." A young woman with slacks and a button-up shirt stopped in front of Ellie. "Is your dog drinking coffee?"

"Mind your own business," Ellie spat.

The plump young woman with brown hair and too much makeup scoffed. "Caffeine can lead to caffeine toxicity in dogs, which can result in—"

"I said mind your own business!" Ellie picked up her dried muffin and tossed it at the woman.

Louie stood, no longer preoccupied with his muffin and latte.

The woman reeled back and inspected her shirt where the muffin hit. "What the hell? That's going to stain. You know what, you psycho? I'm going to call animal control."

"Do it," Ellie shouted. Her last nerve was completely frayed. "I dare you."

"I will!" The woman turned away, mumbling continued threats.

"And if you bug us again, I know where to find plenty of shitty muffins to throw at you!" With one leg crossed over the other, Ellie sipped her latte and stewed in her irritations. "I hate Boston."

"It's not as fun as television made it out to be." Louie grabbed his muffin and set it in her lap.

The two finished their breakfast with a nice cuddle on the bench. As much as she groaned about how awful this adventure was, she wasn't ready to go back home.

After that, they explored building after tall building, car after car, park after park. Their wanderings brought them to the aquarium, which looked like fun, but that would have been an adventure for her alone, and that wasn't an option for her. The museum of fine arts also didn't appreciate canine companionship.

After a long day of disappointment, Ellie and Louie found themselves back at the park. Far from the oak of the mourning woman, they found an unoccupied, bushy area to set up their tent.

"Are you sure you want to sleep out here?" Louie asked as he grabbed the stakes out of the backpack.

"I don't think we have much of a choice, buddy. If muffins and coffee cost thirty bucks, I'd hate to see what a hotel room costs."

It didn't take long to set up the small, one-person tent. Unfortunately, the sunset and horizon were blocked by the city skyline. Stars in the night sky weren't visible either, but they could see something far off in the distance blink as it floated slowly away.

Ellie and Louie sat on the small, inflatable bedroll and nibbled on some provisions they had brought from home. As Ellie crunched on the trail mix, she found herself missing the dinner table, Louie's booster pillow, and that dumb little red bowl. Connecticut, the comforts of home, pulled at her.

After dinner, Ellie sought comfort from Louie. He cuddled up inside the sleeping bag beside her, and only their heads popped out of the cocoon structure. A deep, dreamless sleep took Ellie.

"Get out of there!" A rough, unfriendly voice broke through Ellie's sleep. Bright, unforgiving lights shone on the edge of the tent. Something like a stick smacked the side and startled them.

Louie growled.

What in the Void?

"Get that mutt under control!"

"Then stop hitting the tent," Ellie snapped and felt the hairs on the back of her neck raise as quick zaps of static ran over her. Disheveled, Ellie crawled out of the sleeping bag. Cautiously, she unzipped the first layer of the tent. Two discourteous bright flashlights beamed back at her, blinding her. "Can I help you?"

"You can't camp in the park! The mayor put out a ban before winter," the dark figure on the right said. "There are plenty of beds at the Sisters of Mercy Shelter."

"Sorry, we didn't know. We just got into—"

"I don't need your story. Just pack it up and move along." One of the figures stepped far enough out of the way of the beam that she could see it was a police officer. "You have ten minutes before we'll tear this down for you."

"Okay, okay, we're moving." Ellie zipped the tent back up.

"What's happening?" Louie whispered as he helped her pack up.

"Cops are kicking us out of here." In her frantic, sleepy state, Ellie managed to spill some trail mix inside the tent as well as the envelope her father gave her. Louie picked up the envelope for her as she shoveled trail mix back inside the plastic baggy. Frazzled, they packed up the tent before the officers came back.

"What do you think he meant by there being beds at the Sisters of Mercy Shelter?" Louie asked as Ellie tied the rope back to his collar.

"It sounds like a homeless shelter or something." Ellie yawned.

"But we aren't homeless; we're camping. We should save those beds for people who aren't as lucky as us."

"Tell that to them," she grumbled as they walked.

The exhausted pair found themselves a cozy spot at the enclosed bus stop on the far northern side of the park. Ellie pulled out the cell phone her father gave her and checked the time on the front display of the old flip phone. It was past two in the morning.

"Maybe five hours," she grumbled to herself.

"What's that?" Louie adjusted the backpack so they could lay against it before he climbed up on Ellie.

"We got five hours of sleep." She laid her head back against the plexiglass enclosure. She knew she couldn't fall asleep in such an exposed location, but the moment of quiet was nice.

"Are you thinking about calling home?" Louie asked as Ellie snapped the flip phone shut.

"No, just checking the time." *Tempting though.*

"It's night."

"I got that," she added unenthusiastically. "Hey, buddy, what did you do with that envelope?"

Louie bumped the side pocket of the backpack with his paw.

Dad... As Ellie pulled out the envelope her father prepared for her departure, she thought of his warm smile, goofy laugh, and comforting presence. Even though he betrayed her trust, she still missed all of that.

Her thumb pulled the envelope open, and she found a large stack of money. "No way!"

"What is it?" Louie used her elbow for leverage and pulled up his slinky-like body. "Oh wow!"

"There's a lot of money in here." She flipped through the layers of bills. Affording food or a hotel wouldn't be such a massive blow to their budget anymore. "Come on, buddy. Let's get a good night's sleep."

14

Comfort

No dogs allowed," the young man with an unfortunate abundance of acne, a five o'clock shadow, and dark bags under his eyes behind the counter abruptly informed them. "And we don't accept cash. Company policy—you must have a credit or debit card."

Leave Louie outside next time, then sneak him in. Got it. She hated being dishonest, but this was ridiculous.

"How can you not accept cash?" The words erupted from her lips.

"Company policy," he repeated with the slightest hint of annoyance in his tone. "So, people can't skip out on damages."

"I'm not going to damage anything," Ellie sharply informed him.

"I don't know that, and corporate doesn't know that." He pointed toward the ceiling behind him, where a small, black, bulbous camera hung from the ceiling. With his voice lower, he said, "Want a tip? Try a mom-and-pop shop. They don't have corporate overlords telling them how to breathe and when to eat. Apparently, eating chips when no one is around is some sort of 'offense' punishable by 'termination.'"

Creepy.

It was close to three in the morning now. Hopes of a good night's rest seemed pointless, no matter how much her body and mind begged for it.

"Thanks," Ellie grumbled and dragged herself out of the hotel. On her way out, she observed signs and a concierge station. "They can't afford 'damages' to a room but can afford free pens and wi-fi."

Louis's nails clicked against the stone tile floor of the luxurious lobby as they exited.

"How do I even know if it is a mom-and-pop hotel?" Ellie complained loudly to Louie as they walked in the cool morning air. Even in late spring, the nights were brisk in New England.

Louie and Ellie were not the only ones out on the streets in the pre-twilight hours. They passed people not much older than Ellie, who smelled heavily of booze, others who smelled like garbage, and some who seemed distracted by things far away.

Louie and Ellie strolled back down the road until they found their motorcycle parked in the same spot they had left it; only now, it was accompanied by a hideous bright-orange envelope shoved under the windshield wiper.

Violation
Boston

Ellie's hopes, patience, and heart crumbled beneath her like a champagne tower hit by a cannonball. She didn't quiver or tremble. Ellie exploded into heavy sobs.

"This is... my life. Don't even... I paid... and no dogs? Why?" Her disconnected words fell from her lips with the force of a firehose.

"Oh, Ellie." Louie lifted his front paws and rested them on her leg. "Sweet Ellie, come here."

"It's not fair," she cried loudly. "I didn't know!"

"I know." His head rubbed against her thigh. "It's going to be okay. I promise you."

"Ho-how can you p-promise th-th-that?" Her voice quivered with her sobs.

"Because I love you, and as long as I am by your side, I will—"

"I know." Ellie had heard his devotions before—promises of love, companionship, and protection. Hugging her best friend close, Ellie sank onto the sidewalk, and Louie affectionately wrapped his tiny legs around her the best he could.

"It hasn't been easy."

"No! They're all so mean," she squeaked. "And I paid to park here! This is bullshit!"

Ellie cried and cried until all the sorrow, frustration, and heartbreak from their bumpy start bled out of her system.

"Everything's so hard." She cried into his fuzzy side, "Driving, seeing the city, it's like every corner I turn, someone is yelling at me, or I'm running into a roadblock."

"You can't let this derail you, my dear Ellie. You're much stronger than all of this. I know it all seems hopeless and like the world is cruel, but we can find our place."

"I can't even find a place to sleep." She pouted.

"I—"

An unfamiliar voice interrupted their conversation. "We've gotta place you c'n stay."

Ellie lifted her head and looked over her shoulder at a tall man with shallow cheeks and eyes that looked sickly, even in the darkness. The lanky stranger looked normal in his jeans and thin coat, but something about him made the hairs on the back of Ellie's neck stand on end. His partner, a shorter, portly man, hung back in the shadows.

"We're okay, thanks," Ellie mumbled dismissively and turned her attention back to Louie.

Louie was not so trusting to turn his back on a potential enemy. He poked his head around Ellie.

"You just said you didn't have a place to go. Didn't she, Trev? Am I mishearin' the words that left this girl's mouf?"

The overweight man in the shadows grumbled in agreement.

"Are you sayin' you're too good f'r our place?" His offense to her declination seemed over the top and made every hair on Ellie's body rise with discomfort. She was suddenly aware of every breath that left her lungs and every sound from the city around her.

"No, no, I didn't mean offense, sorry."

"Then come on, we've got a nice bed f'r you, food—"

Sand crunched against the pavement behind her as the stranger took a step toward her. A deep, primal growl rumbled within Louie's throat. She had never heard him make such a threatening noise before—not with Mee-Maw and not even with the police earlier that night.

"You better quiet your mutt."

"Not a mutt." The words left Ellie's lips without her permission. Then, she added, "And not a dog."

Louie moved like a crack of lightning. By the time she got up and turned around, Louie was hanging from the stranger's hand. The man screamed wildly and tried to get the dog off him.

"Don't just stand there, you moron," the leader ordered.

His sidekick emerged from the shadows and beelined towards Ellie. Fear gripped her and froze her in place. *He's massive. He could squish me if he fell on me.*

He stepped again.

But he's slow.

And again.

He can't use magic.... If Louie can be brave, so can I.

Like the brutes in football, she dropped down into a crouched position and charged toward the man. Her hands and legs were primed and ready. He hit like a boulder and pushed Ellie back towards her bike with his impact. Her hands dug into his thick sides.

Please, Void, Seer, be with me.

She sent the most concentrated zap she could into him. Clicks and snaps of electricity filled the air around them as her hair stood on end. The back of her neck ached and sent out a gasp from her lips.

"Ah—" The man backed away from her with wide eyes.

Ellie rubbed the base of her neck and stretched out her jaw as she tried to discharge the extra electricity running through her.

A loud thud rang against the iron gates behind them. Louie no longer dangled from the thin man's hand. Instead, crimson dripped from his palm onto the sidewalk.

No!

"What the hell are you doing?" the injured man shouted as he held his hand.

"She shocked me!" the plump one whined and pointed a finger at Ellie.

"Don' be such a baby!" Just as he finished saying that, a shriek left his lips. Ellie spotted Louie biting his calf.

I need more power. I need more of a source.

Ellie's eyes glanced to the lamp above, then over to her bike.

I don't know where the battery is.

"Will you screw off?" the fat one shouted and landed a kick to Louie's side. The basset hound was torn away by the surprise blow. His long frame skidded across the pavement and ended with a roll. "Tha's more like it."

"Louie!" Ellie gasped. The sheer horror of seeing her best friend, her Familiar, in pain on his side paralyzed her. *Not him.*

The plump one spat a wad of spit at Louie.

A deep, unfiltered hatred ran through Ellie. Along her spine, a surge of electricity danced. The crest of her head tingled as her hands balled into fists. The sensation in her neck felt like something was going to burst.

"Enough!" A deep, familiar voice rumbled from her right and reverberated through her like an avalanche. Out of the corner of her eyes, something bright, red, yellow, and blinding rose from the cold, gray pavement like the tentacle of an ancient, great beast. Its body was composed of molten lava.

"Wha' da hell?"

The amorphous, tentacle-like figure began to take shape. One long, thick branch broke off the bottom and formed into the impression of a leg. The top curled in on itself, resembling the head of a person. Then, shoulders formed, followed by a torso.

The imitation of a strong, human-like form took a cautious step forward; then, it faltered and caught itself. After a moment, it centered itself, and with one long stride, it launched forward. Its arms, like thick bars, hit both men across their midsections, launching them down the length of the sidewalk. Ellie watched the men skid, and then their legs tumbled back over their heads.

They didn't move.

The molten core rapidly cooled and committed to the human form. "Are you alright?" the familiar voice asked.

Beneath the street lights stood a young man with a strong jawline, suave, shaggy hair, rounded shoulders, long, powerful legs, and strong hands. She had never seen this man before, yet he looked so familiar.

He turned around to face her and stepped closer.

Those eyes. Deep, dark-brown eyes that could negotiate a slice of pizza from a homeless man.

"Louie?"

15

Ripples

Ever since her Becoming Ceremony, Ellie had someone profound in her life—Louie. He was a helpful, kind, cuddly friend in the form of an adorable basset hound! Everything she could ever need or want was pre-packaged in the most perfect, wide-footed, droopy-eyed form. He was her rock. Childish fears that went bump in the night, he chased them away. Because of him, threats like bees couldn't even get close to Ellie. At the end of a difficult day, he always knew how to put a big smile on her face. Whether that meant he would cross his paws in a dapper manner and puff out his brilliant white chest, stand on her lap and give her big puppy eyes, or tackle and smother her with kisses. Louie was her shimmer of hope and light when the dark was at its darkest.

What sideshow of fate is this?

But now, in the early morning hours, a stranger sat beside her—a handsome stranger in a chunky, boxy, 1970s purple and chrome sidecar seat—without a helmet—where the basset hound sat the night before. Flappy cheeks were replaced by a bearded smile. Unruly ears were replaced by blond strands of hair. The slinky-like frame with clumsy paws and an oddly proportioned chest was now a tall, muscular young man with broad shoulders.

The worst part of all of this, beyond the possible dead bodies on the sidewalk, the chaos of their day in Boston, and the lack of sleep hit Ellie. *He's really good-looking.*

Ellie could no longer look at Louie and feel calm, centered, happy, and cozy. Now, when she looked at him, her chest fluttered, and her stomach felt lighter.

What's wrong with you? He's your Familiar! He literally just put his life on the line for you, maybe even killed two people, and you're acting like a love-struck schoolgirl? You're nineteen! Get it together! She scolded herself again and again. *You have a prophecy of death floating over your head, and you can't even keep your thoughts straight? Your eyes on the road? You're pathetic.*

Anytime Louie caught one of her stolen glances, he'd smile and wave.

No matter how many times she looked at him, the sensation didn't fade. Part of her wished it was a dream, and she'd wake up in the tent in the park—or even in their bed back in Connecticut.

The twinkle of city lights rapidly disappearing in the rearview mirror brought a sense of relief to Ellie. *Never again,* she promised herself as the Honda rumbled and roared beneath her frame. *Boston is done.* They traveled down the nearly empty, multi-lane highway toward their new destination, Cape Cod.

They passed through small towns and big cities, which looked abandoned in the twilight hours. Pine-ladened woods acted as the genesis of the Cape Cod peninsula. Well-groomed roads soon gave way to a bumpy, two-laned highway. Highly populated exits yielded to tight turn-offs and mom-and-pop shops. Ellie was comforted by the shadows of treetops that stood higher than the buildings peeking out of the foliage.

After thirty minutes along the northbound road, the lazy sun threatened the retreating night sky, and their headlights fell on a large, green street sign that read Nauset Beach, with an arrow pointing to the right.

The promise of beach, ocean, waves, and sand was all Ellie needed to pull them off course. Without hesitation, she steered the motorcycle down the side road toward the coast.

It took a few minutes for the shadow-plagued trees of Beach Road to finally drop away and reveal the small stretch of sky before them. Desperation overtook her, and her hand heavily pulled on the throttle. She couldn't explain it, but Ellie just had to get to the horizon. She *had* to watch the sunrise on the beach this morning.

With the final stretch of road before them, a slight bend to the right revealed a petite information shack beside a stop sign and metal guards. She read the signs.

No Lifeguard on Duty
Area Closed from 11 p.m. to 6 a.m.

"Shove it," Ellie sneered as the wide-set motorbike puttered through the nearly empty parking lot. They defiantly ignored the yellow directional arrows on the old pavement and drove directly to the entrance where beach sand overtook the pavement, and flimsy wooden fences guided them toward the entrance. Large signs stood before the it, but Ellie didn't have time for those.

The sun threatened to break the skyline now. Gentle yellows and reds lined the horizon, guiding her eyes to where the sun would poke out. Her stupid, thick motorcycle helmet was tight and hot against her head.

Get it off, get it off! Ellie stepped away from the motorcycle as her chilled fingers fumbled with the thick fabric straps.

"What's wrong?" Louie's new, dreamy, somewhat familiar deep voice tried to get her attention as she scrambled with the helmet.

You're not Louie. That thought came with a heaping tablespoon of guilt in her stomach. Tears and adrenaline threatened her as she finally got the straps to give-way. The helmet let out a crunchy cracking sound as it hit the pavement. Ellie took off in a sprint toward the water.

"Ellie, slow down," Louie called from the motorcycle.

She yearned to feel the salt water before the sun broke the horizon—she just had to watch the sunrise while in the ocean.

I need one good first, just one on this awful trip. The sand beneath her feet gave way with every step.

"Are you okay?" Not a paw, but a hand touched the back of Ellie's forearm. His voice was just over her shoulder.

"No!" The word erupted from her mouth. She pulled away from his touch and ripped off her shoes and socks. They fell to the beach, and she ran further.

Sand grew firmer and wetter beneath her feet as she approached the tide. In a beautiful rhythm, the clear, ice-cold water rumbled forward to her feet. The brief sensation wasn't enough, though. Ellie trudged deeper until the water rushed over her feet, and soon, she was in the frigid cold waters up to her ankles. Tears of relief built up in her eyes as she took in the gorgeous sunrise.

The bright, welcoming light of the red sun cracked over the horizon. As she inhaled, her breath caught in her chest against a sob. A tremendous sense of heartbreak and relief washed over Ellie as her chest trembled with anxiety. Exhausted and with barely any tears left to give, Ellie huffed weary breaths. From over her shoulder, she felt Louie's presence.

"Sweet Ellie, what's wrong?" he asked in a soft tone.

"You!" She pointed at him. "This! Everything!"

Louie winced.

She never wanted to hurt him. *He doesn't deserve this.*

"I mean, why?" The words finally left her lips. "Why this? Why aren't you a basset hound anymore? Why?"

The hurt young man took a step back to consider her words. Louie held out his arms and looked down the length of them; then, he checked his core. "Did I not do a good job?"

That completely threw Ellie off.

"I-I thought this was a good balance. I used the guys from the stores you like."

"What?" Her face twisted with confusion and frustration.

"The clothing stores? The magazines your mom has." Worry was prominent on his face. "Your eyes always linger on the guys with the beards and thick legs."

"Oh my gods." Ellie covered her face with her hands. She wanted to hide, to find a rock, something, anything to curl up under and die! He had noted the kinds of guys she found attractive. "What the hell? Why?"

Everybody else around me gets to have secrets, but not me. Not Ellie!

When she managed to look up from her hands, all she could see was the pained look on Louie's face. She wanted to embrace him and take it all away. "No, no, it's not your looks. You did great."

Louie's expression eased. His eyebrows softened. "Then what'd I do?"

"You changed," she said. "Why? Why'd you change? It's like... you're not, not—"

"Your dog?" He looked down.

"No," Ellie snapped. *Yes!* He wasn't her adorable, sweet, clumsy little basset hound anymore. *You're as shallow as the rest of them.* Ellie ran her hands through her hair. *All of the fights with mom, Mee-Maw. In the end, he was just your pet—not your equal, you hypocrite.*

"Ellie, you know you're the most important person in the world to me. My meaning, my purpose—I need to keep you safe and happy."

Declarations of his devotion were normal, but when the words left a man's mouth, they sounded much sweeter than they did coming from a dog.

"I just think I reached my usefulness as your pet."

"You weren't—"

"In the eyes of the world, I was," he reminded her. "Because of me, you couldn't sleep safely in a hotel. Because of me, you couldn't enjoy your first latte in a cafe like you always dreamed of."

Ellie let out a weary sigh.

"Those creeps approached you because they thought you were alone, an easy target."

"How do you know?" Ellie challenged.

"Be practical here. You were young, alone, and crying in the middle of the night— and hugging a small dog." Louie took a step towards her. Now, with him beside her in the chilled water, she noticed just how wide his frame was and how tall he was in comparison to her.

This is too much.

"Well, you said you could change into anything, like a manatee, re-member? You could have been a rottweiler or a-a German Shep—"

"You don't like either of those breeds," he reminded her. "And try to get a room with a manatee? Come on."

His words hung in the air around them.

Being a person does make a lot of sense, and well... he nailed it, right down to the red-and-black flannel shirt.

"Maybe, in a few months, when you're happy and settled down, we could find a nice little place, and I could turn back into a basset hound—or one of those flat-faced ones." Louie held a hand up to his nose to demonstrate it.

"Pug," Ellie reminded him. "But I don't like the idea of you chang-ing forms so... so thoughtlessly."

"Does this look thoughtless?" Louie lifted his left hand and wiggled his thumb.

Ellie went to speak, sighed, and rolled her eyes. "You know what I mean."

"I guess I don't," Louie admitted.

"Like, I don't.... I don't like the idea of you changing your form be-cause you think it's what I want or like. I-I want you to change it for *you.*"

Ellie looked out at the rolling waves.

"Despite what Mee-Maw believes, you weren't made to *serve* me. I want you to be your own person, be you, be who I love and adore! I want you to have your own dreams, opinions, likes, and dislikes!"

Ellie's voice grew as she continued with the list.

"Whatever, whoever instilled that within you..." Ellie waved her hands before her. "Begone. It's gone. You be yourself. Be your own person. Stop trying to please me all the time."

Louie took a step away from Ellie. His face contorted with confusion.

Ellie breathlessly took in his expression. "Louie, I didn't mean to hurt you. I—"

Louie turned away from Ellie and trudged back through the chilly water toward the sandy beach.

"Lou—"

He lifted his hand, hung his head low, and took a seat on the sand.

Before them, the deep-red sun rose over the horizon and greeted the world with a fiery brightness.

We made it. She sighed with relief before she looked back to her distraught Familiar. She waded through the waves toward the shore.

Louie buried his head in his arms, and Ellie took a seat beside him.

"Do you want me to go back to The Void?" Louie asked in a hushed tone.

"What? No!" Ellie placed her hand against his lower back. "No, no, no. Why do you think that?"

"You just... you dismissed me." He lifted his head, and the loose blond bangs hung over his eyes, obscuring those deep brown eyes she loved. "I've failed as a Familiar."

Ellie wrapped her arms around him in a tight hug. "You have not!" She held him tight. "No, no, no. You're the best Familiar. My best friend."

"Then why did you tell me to stop?" Louie retreated into her hug. "I live for you."

"Louie." She affectionately ran her hand up the length of his back and rested her head against his. He was so large, she had to perch on her knees. "I want you to live *with* me—not *for* me."

Louie lifted his head to look up to her.

"I want you to be my equal, my partner, my best friend at my side." She gently smiled. "I don't want anybody in our new life thinking you're my slave or meant to serve me or anything like that."

Those deep brown eyes reflected the beautiful sunlight behind her. She planted a loving, tender kiss on his forehead.

"I love you," she reminded him. "I always want you with me."

"I love you, too."

Ellie rested her head on top of Louie's. Behind them, the sun continued to rise, and the waves crashed.

"What's that?" Louie asked with his head just over her shoulder. A finger extended out towards a bulbous, dark object that broke the surface of the water. It bobbed with the waves for a few moments before it sank below once again.

"What was that?" She pulled away from the hug and studied the waves.

"Definitely not a hermit crab," Louie muttered.

A chuckle left Ellie's lips. "Well, yeah, dummy."

It didn't resurface for a few minutes. When it finally did, they watched as it came into view amongst the light of sunrise. It looked like a fat cork bouncing around the rolling tide. It was a seal.

"Can I admit something to you?" Ellie's voice was now just above a whisper, like she didn't want to frighten the creature.

"Always." Louie offered her his hand as he stood.

She took it and joined him in a walk along the surf. "I hate Boston."

As they weaved between the wet and dry sand of the tide, Ellie spilled out every little grievance she had—from the overly manicured trees to the smell of the hotel's lobby.

"Well, we never have to go back."

"Never, ever," Ellie confirmed and sat back in the dry sand.

Seeing Ellie's tired shoulders and tense jaw relaxed, Louie walked out to the water while she rested in the sand.

She watched Louie's tall frame meander the surf. Ellie pulled her riding jacket up and closed her eyes. The sound of the waves as they rhythmically rolled in and receded back toward the depths lulled her into a relaxed state.

It seemed like a long blink when she finally opened her eyes and saw that the sun had fully risen. Warmth covered her body. By her feet, Louie had constructed a sandcastle with a moat the tide filled and emptied with each wave. He tediously decorated the columns and walkways with small shells, rocks, and sticks. When he made eye contact with Ellie, he happily took his place next to her.

"I got you something."

"Hm?" Ellie sat up and adjusted her jacket. Sand slid down her back beneath her shirt and into her pants. She grimaced and writhed at the sensation.

From his shorts pocket, Louie pulled out a white, clean-looking shell. It was oval-shaped and had a rough edge to it. Gentle ripples decorated it from the top of the neck down to the outer edges. The inside of the shell had a gentle, smooth gloss. It was simple and beautiful.

"I love it."

"I thought, maybe it could represent this part of our journey? Every time you look at it, you'll be reminded of this sunrise and how the waves sounded and felt. This moment when we came back together, when everything was so tough."

The beautiful, simple shell sat inside of her palm, and a smile crept across her lips. *That's my Louie. He's more than a basset hound or a manatee. He's a kind, lovely soul.* She pulled him into a tight embrace.

It was fulfilling and sweet to have actual arms hugging her back, and it felt different from a hug she'd get from her mom, dad, or any relative. This hug had so much strength and promise to it. Finally, she managed to pull herself away.

"We need to keep this safe," she finally said.

They stayed at the beach until Ellie's stomach beckoned them to find something to eat. They made their way back up the sand, through the wooden fences, and toward the parking lot. Now, in the light of day, Ellie could see they weren't just plain signs. One was a bulletin board flooded with local advertisements for babysitters, lawn mowing, help wanted, cars for sale, apartments for rent, and missing persons. She also saw one massive, official warning sign.

Warning
Great White Sharks hunt seals in shallow waters at this beach

"Oh wow." Ellie's mouth was wide open as she looked at the sign, shocked.

"What?"

"Great White Sharks hunt in these waters."

With that, Louie put a protective arm around Ellie. A gentle tug toward the parking lot made her chuckle. Of course, she playfully fought back and stepped daringly toward the beach.

"Don't even think about it," he warned as they walked back to the bike.

16

Familiar

The purple and chrome Honda made it back to the main road that stretched along the length of Cape Cod. Their detour to Nauset Beach landed them in the small town of Orleans. The cozy town was barely awake in the shimmers of twilight. The only stoplights they ran into flashed yellow instead of the full trio of red, yellow, and green. Stores still had their open signs unlit, and very few cars passed. There was an odd abundance of putt-putts, ice cream, and lobster shacks.

Bagels, eggs, and vanilla lattes played on repeat in Ellie's mind. *My stomach is going to eat itself if I don't get something substantial into it.* As they proceeded through Orleans, store after store remained closed. *Please, please let something be open.*

They made it out of Orleans and passed signs for Eastham and Wellfleet. Each town was just like Orleans, sleepy and desolate. When all hope seemed lost, amongst the coniferous trees as tall as buildings and bountiful shrubbery, the Sugar Shack emerged, standing out like a sore thumb.

It was a bright-yellow and white restaurant designed to look like someone tried to shrink a house and turn it into a modest diner. A pristine white porch complete with railings and decorative support beams boasted the dark metal numbers—**4022**. Instead of stairs up to the porch, a ramp made of planks enticed guests of all abilities to enter. A huge rocking chair sat off to the left on the windowless side of the porch. It was comically large, given the size of the area it occupied. Gorgeous blue, white, and orange flowers speckled the background of the chair—surely, this was set up for tourists to take adoring family photographs. A small hand-painted sign mounted to the wall to the right of the frame read:

Sugar Shack
Wellfleet, MA

On the right-hand side of the porch was a little window with white siding. Blue curtains on the inside of the building were tied back so people could look in and out. The specials board, a black chalk board mounted to a wooden frame, sat on the porch. Each special was written in beautiful cursive yellow chalk:

Lobster Benedict $10
Sugar Stack $5
Bubba's Breakfast Sandwich $4, add bacon $0.50
Hours: Monday–Sunday 5:00 a.m.–2 p.m.

Lobster benedict? Ellie cringed as she killed the engine of the motorcycle. After the abundance of putt-putts and ice cream shops that boasted world-famous lobster rolls, she had lost her desire to try the crustacean. *If lobsters go extinct in this century, we know who to blame, Cape Cod.*

A beautiful basket hung next to the white-framed window below a black metal porch light. Stunning nasturtium plants trailed down the front of the basket with their unique, circular green leaves and bright-orange blossoms. German chamomile stood tall in the background with its tiny yellow centers and bright-white petals. A sage plant burst from the far right in the middle height, accompanied by a gorgeous little mound of marigolds.

"Louie." Ellie gave him a nudge with the back of her hand. He looked over at the basket and gave a happy *Ohh*. "I can hear Mom now."

"A witch is nothing without a good clump of sage," Louie playfully mocked, like they did back at home.

Ellie pulled open the front door and led them inside. The Sugar Shack was a tiny establishment. It looked like it was mostly set up for people who wanted to come and go. One older gentleman was tucked away in a comfy, plush, green chair in the far-left corner, reading a newspaper. A bagel and a cup of coffee sat on the small end table to his right. Ellie saw two empty morning breakfast nook seats by the windows on the far edges of the room. A sign hung on the wall and pointed down a narrow hallway to the right of the counter which read:

Bathrooms
&
Extra Seating

Before them was a beautiful glass display case filled with gorgeous homemade strudel, scones, and a variety of muffins. A plump older woman with a wide, genuine smile, curly gray hair, and thick glasses stood behind the counter. She wore an apron covered with floury handprints and had a blue pen mark along her cheek, the culprit of which was stuck behind her right ear.

"Good morning! First time here?"

"Yes." For the first time in days, Ellie didn't feel an overwhelming sense of grief to speak with someone behind a register.

"Welcome! Welcome! We have a few extra tables out back, and you're just in time to beat the morning rush! Fresh coffee is brewing—local beans. Will you be dining in with us or taking it on the road?"

"In," Louie answered from behind.

Ellie jerked her head back and looked at the handsome bearded man to her right.

"Please? I like it here."

A smile crept across Ellie's face as those brown eyes pleaded with her. *He's still got it.*

"I do, too." She nodded to the woman behind the register. "In, please."

"Let's get you two seated! The back porch is just lovely right now. I'll meet you at the end of that hallway." She gestured to the signs on the wall and disappeared into the kitchen behind her.

"In, please," Ellie playfully mocked Louie.

"Meh, meh, meh." Louie returned the mocking as they walked towards the hallway made narrower by bookshelves loaded with board games, plants, and knick-knacks. Ellie stepped forward and ran into Louie's firm arm. This sense of warmth welcomed her to stay close. She wanted to wrap her arms around his bicep, hug him close, and enjoy his comforting presence. *He doesn't smell half bad, either.*

"Oh, sorry." Louie chuckled and took a step back. He gestured for her to go first. "So used to squeezing next to you, just didn't think."

"Thanks." Ellie awkwardly ducked into the hallway.

"Sorry, it's a bit of a tight squeeze," the woman said as she opened the door and walked them outside. "I just can't bring myself to get rid of my bookshelves. Even if my old junk brings a smile to one family's face on a rainy day, I figure it's worth it."

A little wooden porch with a small table and two seats sat far away from the sounds of the kitchen and the smells of the bathroom. It was enclosed by white lattice, which already had morning glories along it. The roof of the porch extended out over a small garden.

The ground was made of decorative stones held together by fine sand. A small, house-shaped structure made of pallets and decorated by yellow siding encapsulated more seating. Off the porch, benches lined the interior of the half-height walls. White lattice alternated with open space and gave the impression of an enclosed building. Bright-yellow support beams held up the shingle-covered roof.

"This is beautiful," Ellie exclaimed as they were led out to a small table with one chair and an opening on the bench.

"Oh, thank you. Our grandson put it together for us. Such a sweet boy."

Both sides of the menu were set into the tabletop, along with pressed flowers and beautiful stones.

"Is this glass?" Ellie asked as her hand danced over the shimmering top.

"Oh no, resin, I think. Each table is unique and handmade." She adjusted her pants. "My name's Mary. Can I start you off with some coffee?"

Coffee. Coffee. Coffee. It was like music to Ellie's ears.

"So much coffee." She chuckled.

"Okay." Mary let out a chuckle as she made a note in her small notepad. "It sounds like you need one of our big mugs. And you, sir?"

"Oh, um, yeah." Louie looked down at the table awkwardly, his hands spread out over the resin top. "Coffee sounds good."

"He likes lots of cream in his coffee, so could you bring—"

"My son's the same way." Mary waved her hand, not needing further explanation, before she turned. "May as well bring the cow; am I right?"

Ellie snickered and looked at Louie, who just seemed happy to be there. As soon as the screen door of the back porch slammed shut, Ellie announced, "I think I adore her. Do you think she's a witch?"

"Could be. She's charming," he admitted before he turned his attention to the beautiful world around them.

Ellie focused on the menu. They had everything: eggs, pancakes, pastries, omelets. A dinner of trail mix before such a stress-filled night really took the energy out of her. "I'm so hungry, I need something that'll stick to me."

The screen door squeaked, and Mary came out with a shallow black tray. Steam danced above the mugs before her.

"The hummingbirds love it around here," she explained to Louie as she placed the cups of coffee in front of them. "Just wait until August when everything is in bloom. You can't keep them away."

Ellie was so wrapped up in the food choices she hadn't even noticed the small, busy bird as it fluttered and zipped from flower to flower along the lattice. She followed Mary and Louie's gaze up to the bright-red feeder in the center of the seating area.

"I'll be back in a minute for your order."

Ellie's cup of coffee was more like a soup bowl with a tiny handle on the edge. *Perfect.* Louie had a large, low coffee cup, but it must have been their "normal" size compared to what Ellie had. Mary left plenty of room for cream and sugar in his.

"Do you know what you want?" Ellie asked as she fixed her cup of coffee.

Louie shrugged and didn't bother to look at the menu as he made his cup.

"Maybe you should look at the menu instead of the flowers?"

"Why?" Louie looked down at the menu on his side of the table.

Ellie raised her eyebrows. "So you can pick out what you'd like to order."

Why do I have to spell it out for him? Then again, they didn't really go out to places that often, and when they did, Ellie usually ordered for him. A basset hound placing an order would certainly end up on the news.

"I can't read, Ellie."

Those words hit like a punch to her gut. *How could I have never noticed that before?*

"Are you okay?" Louie asked from across the table.

"Just shoot me now." Ellie groaned into her hands, and she doubled over onto the table. "Take me out back and put a bullet in my head. I'm done."

"What'd I do?" The chair squeaked, but before she could stop him, a hand was on her back, and Louie was at her side. *Of course—I insult him, and he's comforting me.*

"Nothing, you're great! I just—I embarrassed myself."

"Oh! Oh!" He bounced beside her. "Um, what'd your dad call this? A toe mouth?"

"Foot-in-mouth moment," she reminded him and tried to shake off her embarrassment.

"No need to be embarrassed, Ellie. Not like it's ever been brought up before."

Ellie tried to shake it off, but her traitorous cheeks flushed. The quick kiss to the top of her head didn't help at all. Frozen in place, she asked, "Why'd you do that?"

"Do what?" Louie's attention was already back to the humming-birds.

"Kiss me."

"I always give you kisses."

Kisses, she thought. *Licks, cuddling, sitting in my lap...* Her mind flooded with the memories of the basset hound snuggled inside of the sleeping bag with her—Ellie's arms wrapped around him, his nose beneath her chin. Now, the droopy-faced, fat dog was replaced by this young man. Her cheeks grew warmer as her hands became damp.

Louie pulled his attention from the hummingbird and looked back at her. His fingers tucked an unruly curly hair back behind her ear.

Those brown eyes studied her face like they had a million times before, but the way it made her feel was unlike anything she had ever felt. Her breath shook when she exhaled.

"Are you feeling okay?" He tilted his head slightly to the side. "You're all flushed and sweaty."

"I'm fine!" Ellie pulled away from him and took her massive mug in her hand. She brought the hot liquid to her lips and chugged it down. *What's wrong with you? How can you look at him like that? He's your best friend. You can't do that! Just focus on breakfast.* "Um, do you know what you want?"

"I'm not picky." Those big shoulders shrugged nonchalantly.

"I know, but you probably don't want more muffins, right?"

"I like muffins."

"I know," she repeated. "But would you prefer to have eggs this morning or pancakes?"

"Eggs," he said firmly. "It's only Tuesday. Pancakes are for Saturdays."

Ellie bit her lip to hold back her smile. "Alright then."

Together, they went through the options before they settled on which breakfasts to order. Scrambled eggs, bacon, and Texas toast for Louie. Over-easy eggs, sausage, and rye toast for Ellie. As soon as the orders were out of the way and the two were left to wait with their coffee, she felt that excitement in her stomach once again. She needed something, anything to distract her.

"Think my mom's mad?"

"Not as mad as Mee-Maw will be." Louie smirked. "That jerk is probably—"

Ellie covered her face in fear of spitting out her coffee as she laughed with surprise.

"What?" Louie smiled wide.

"You've never called her that before!" Ellie grabbed a napkin from the table and quickly cleaned up the bit of coffee that managed to get on her hand.

"Was that bad?" His smile didn't fade.

"No, I loved it. She is a jerk."

Obviously eager to keep her smile going, Louie continued. "To answer your question, Kimberly is probably panicking," Louie said as he looked off into the forest beyond them. "Your father's probably comforting her. Impossible to get through to her that you're not already dead."

A creature of darkness. Ellie had completely forgotten about the prophecy with the insanity of the last twenty-four hours.

"Ellie?" Louie tapped the table before her.

Ellie looked up.

"Did I say something wrong?"

"No," she tucked the same strand behind her ear. "I just remembered that prophecy."

"What did it say again?"

The door creaked, and Mary came out with a hot pot of coffee in hand. "Top you off?" she offered.

"Yes, please," Louie answered and leaned back to give her space.

"I left something in my bike. Is it okay if I grab it?" Ellie asked Mary as she switched to top Ellie off.

"Of course, dear."

Ellie returned to the table moments later with Betty Fischer's Diary. Carefully, she flipped the pages until she came to the page with her initials scribbled into the corner.

> *A creature of darkness, of hunger, of longing, and suffering—*
> *a Familiar—lost and alone.*
> *Ellie-Lynne Betty Becker will meet her fate one spring eve.*
> *Pain and temptation.*
> *The Void calls.*
> *Heat.*

"What does it say?" Louie asked.

Ellie read the words to him.

Louie leaned in. "Read it again?"

Ellie did.

"You said this is the diary of Betty Fischer?"

"Yes." Ellie ripped off a bit of napkin and put it in the book as a bookmark.

"To me, and this is just me, it sounds jumbled up, like when you speak with someone who's excited or who can't focus." He sat back up. "It's like the thoughts are bouncing back and forth."

Ellie looked over the words again.

"'The Void calls' part seems out of place. The Void is always calling." Louie took a sip of his coffee. "You all just can't hear it."

"Really? What does it sound like?"

"Kind of like that horn on boats, but much lower. It changes from time to time. Betty told me it's dependent on if it's feeding."

"Betty?"

Just then, the door creaked open, and Mary stepped out with two plates.

Terrible timing. Ellie closed the diary, put it off to the side, and straightened up.

"Eggs and bacon?"

Louie put up his hand. Mary slid his plate in front of him.

"And this must be for you." She put the other plate in front of Ellie. "Can I get you two anything else?"

Ellie calmly shook her head from side to side. Louie mimicked her gesture.

"Well, enjoy! I'll be up front if you need anything."

Louie picked up his fork awkwardly and scooped his eggs onto it. "Ellie, look." He excitedly pulled up eggs. "Fork."

The backdoor shut.

"That's great. Back to our conversation. What do you mean the Void feeds?"

Louie's eggs fell off his fork back onto his plate. He looked at the pile disappointed and tried again. "You know, when people make offerings and sacrifices?"

"People do what?" She leaned over the table with wide eyes.

"Yeah, some people throw food and flowers into the Void." He spoke slowly as he tried to remember his fork lessons from years ago. "Or when... a... clairvoyant goes..."

"Oh my god, Louie." Ellie put her hands out desperately. "Put down the fork and just tell me."

"But I'm hungry." Those brown eyes looked at her with heartbreak.

"Eat the toast. What about clairvoyants?"

Louie took her suggestion and sheepishly explained as he crunched into the thick bread. "When clairvoyants turn marriage age in Oren, they are sent to the Void. Betty told me about it. I guess she was put into a dress and had to walk into a Calling Circle in front of everybody."

"Betty?" Ellie raised an eyebrow and tapped the top of the diary. "Like, this Betty?"

"Yeah! I thought I told you; she's your Seer."

How can he possibly be eating through this? Ellie closed her eyes and exhaled slowly to remain calm. "No, I think you overlooked that detail."

"Sorry." With one extended finger, Louie reached across the table and poked her plate so it was closer to her. "Eat, or your food will get cold."

Ellie sighed and shoved a sausage into her mouth. "Continue."

"Oh, well, it's been a while since she shared the story with me. She, um, she tried to hide her visions so the council wouldn't find out. If I remember correctly, she had a really hard time hiding it the older she got. It was like people, voices, would come to her all at once, and she'd try to sort through them. She said it was hard to stay in the moment. I guess when she got to The Void, the way time works up there, it made it easier for her to listen. Anyway, that's why I think her prophecy sounds jumbled." He nodded to the diary. "It sounds like she was hearing a few different conversations at once."

Ellie tried to sort through what she just learned. "She tried to hide her visions? Didn't they make her put it on display at her Becoming Ceremony?"

"Yeah, I think she said she faked water breathing or something." Louie shrugged. "She told me on our way to your puddle, so it's all a bit fuzzy."

He doesn't remember. She sighed and turned her attention to her plate while her thoughts turned over the information. Lost in thought, she hadn't even realized she had eaten everything until Louie interrupted her.

"Do you want my last piece of toast?" He held out the crusty piece of bread.

"I'm fine." She shook her head and set down her fork. "Just on auto-pilot."

The journal on the table stared at her. To keep her mind from it, Ellie placed it in her lap. "Okay. Let's change the subject. What do you want to do today?"

17

Nerves

E verything." Louie shoved his last piece of toast into his face just as Mary walked back out, now accompanied by a middle-aged couple.

"Helpful." Ellie smirked. "What about First Encounter Beach?"

"We should go during the new moon! I bet it would be cool then." Louie's smile grew wide with wonder. It was contagious.

While they finished their coffees, they passed around ideas.

"Hermit crab hunting?" Louie suggested.

"Hiking?" Ellie countered.

"Putt-putt." Louie nodded down the road.

"We could go swimming at shark beach."

"Absolutely not," Louie protested. "Never on my life."

In the end, they agreed on getting Louie a helmet, riding around the Cape, and maybe trying out putt-putt for the first time.

"Could I interest you two in anything sweet?" Mary asked as she cleared away the plates.

"No thanks," Louie answered first. "I'm watching my figure."

Ellie tried to hide her snicker.

"You? If you say so." Mary chuckled politely.

"Mary, let me ask you something," Louie said, catching her attention before she could get away.

That's an Elijah move right there, Ellie thought as she watched Louie with curious eyes.

"Yes?" Mary stopped mid-pivot.

"Would you happen to know where we might find some hermit crabs?"

Joy lit up her face. "I do! Guaranteed. There's a big restaurant called the Shell Pile in Provincetown, and you can find tons of crabs under the pier next to it. We took our grandson out there every Sunday for fifteen years."

"Same grandson who built this?" Ellie asked.

"One and the same. Only grandson." She offered a friendly smile. "I'll get you two the check so you can get out of here."

When Ellie and Louie got out to the parking lot, they could see the start of the morning rush that Mary predicted. A family with five children, all under the age of ten, walked past them toward the entrance.

"That motorcycle is so pretty," the little girl with blond pigtails cooed as her parents tugged her inside.

"Our bike *is* cool," Ellie mentioned to Louie as she climbed back onto the seat.

"Never doubted that." Louie approached the side car and awkwardly climbed into it with very pointed movements. With his size, he looked like an overfilled muffin top.

Ellie and Louie spent their first day traveling the length of the Cape and learning the layout. They discovered Provincetown, a vibrant coastal town that populated the tip of Cape Cod. Pilgrims First Landing Park, a historical sight, sat in the center of a roundabout. That visit was the product of poor navigation.

In their travels between Orleans and Eastham, they discovered an endearing spot where they could rent a cabin for the night. In Chatham, they visited a small red and white lighthouse accompanied by a boat along the beach.

Ellie's energy for the day faded quickly. Just after four in the afternoon, she was ready to check-in to their cabin. To check-in, they entered a beautiful gray house with white shutters and large bushes populated by promising blue buds. An in-ground pool was enclosed by a chain-linked fence with warning signs.

No Lifeguard On Duty
No Rough Housing

White beach chairs sat inside with a couple of complimentary pool toys. A stretch of matching small cabins extended back into the trees. The caretaker, Craig, was a kind, middle-aged man with a mustache that would be intimidated by Elijah's robust one.

The moment Louie and Ellie stepped inside their cabin, it was as if all the stresses of the last few days melted away—no demands for leashes, no need to sneak Louie in, and, as far as she knew, no creeps in any corners.

"No ghosts or ghouls here," Louie announced as he checked the closet and under the large bed.

The cabin was a studio room with a separate bathroom, a breakfast nook that looked out into the forest, a small kitchenette, and an older television at the foot of a double-sized bed. Ellie dropped her helmet, slid off her jacket, and melted face-first into the comfortable bed.

I can't wait to shower. A tug at her foot forced her to lift her head and look over her shoulder.

"You should get some sleep." Louie tossed her shoe to the floor and made quick work of the second one before he climbed onto the bed. He passed her and went to the pillows, where he began to set them up just how she liked.

"Sleep sounds good." As Louie worked his magic to make the bed comfortable, one of his many appreciated skills, Ellie pulled herself from the plush comforter and hobbled to the breakfast nook. *One last thing.*

With a heavy head, Ellie pulled out the flip phone.

"Lou," she called.

Louie had made himself comfortable on the bed; he looked up from the television.

"Look, there's chickadees."

"Tweet, tweet," he returned, and Ellie's smile grew.

They were his second-most favorite animal to harass in the Connecticut woods. With a deep breath and a roll of her aching shoulders, Ellie dialed their home line.

Ring, ring... Ring—

"Hello?"

She immediately relaxed when she recognized her dad's voice. "Hey, it's Ellie."

"Oh, thank the Void." Elijah let out a sigh of relief. "Sweety, it's been killing me not to hear from you."

"Sorry, I—"

"Don't apologize. I just didn't realize how hard letting the baby bird fly out of the nest is on a parent." Elijah's voice faltered. Ellie wanted to hug him tightly. "How-how is everything? How's the pup?"

"Not a pup anymore." She laughed, and Louie looked over in her direction. With a smile on his face, he wiggled his feet, then turned his attention back to the television.

"Wait, he changed?" Elijah's voice stole her attention again.

Ellie was more than happy to take the opportunity and relive every detail that irritated her about Boston, the crazy people she ran into, and the cost of everything.

When she brought up the men and Louie's change, Elijah snapped, "What?"

Ellie cringed away from the phone.

"I'm sorry, honey. I just... I worry. I'm so happy you're okay to tell me about this. Go on."

She told him about breakfast that morning but left out what she learned about Betty Fischer. *I can keep secrets, too.* Tales of their travels ended with their cozy little cabin overlooking the chickadee-filled forest.

"That's such a relief." He chuckled. "You need to make sure you're taking time out to shower, do your laundry, and eat real food. You can't live off candy."

"Try me," she challenged, and that lightened the mood.

Ellie couldn't make out the mumble in the background, but she knew that voice well. Her mother did *not* sound happy.

"You're in the doghouse?" Ellie asked.

"Don't worry about me," Elijah reassured her. "I'd make the same choice again."

Ellie smiled softly. *Always gotta be my champion.*

"Can I ask one more thing of you, Ellie-Lynne?"

Full name? This is serious.

"Will you call me a little more often? I need to know you're still breathing."

"Yes. I can do that." Ellie shifted her weight in her chair.

"Thank you. I love you. Stay safe."

"Will do. I love you too." With a foot wiggle in her peripheral, Ellie quickly added, "Louie says 'hi.'"

"Tell him I said 'hello, sir.'"

"Oh, and Dad?"

"Yes, honey?"

"I'm still mad at her, but, can you tell Mom I love her?"

"I will, sweetie. And she loves you, too. We both do—more than you'll ever know. Stay safe, and don't forget to call."

Ellie plugged in the phone to let it charge before she returned to bed. "I was going to take a shower, but I don't have the energy."

Louie hummed happily as she climbed into the prepared spot. The extra pillows were on the floor, and two pillows sat side by side. A familiar show played on the television, but the volume was turned down low. A cool breeze from the open window above the bed danced through her hair.

"Sleepy time." Ellie rested her head on one of the pillows, and Louie pulled the blankets around her. It was like a fluffy marshmallow from heaven.

As she lay there, her thoughts and breath began to slow just as a warm weight settled in next to her. Then a weight moved on to her shoulder blade. Ellie turned her head to the side to see Louie's messy hair as he cuddled up on her. Her heart fluttered in her chest, and a rush of nervousness took over.

"Can I help you?" Ellie pulled herself away so his head was no longer on her and she could face him.

Louie's eyebrows drew together as he sunk away. "You don't want to cuddle?"

"Of course—" Her words caught in her throat. *What are you doing? Get a hold of yourself.*

She had never cuddled with someone else, well, a guy, before. The thought had crossed her mind in daydreams or before she fell asleep at night, but she never had the opportunity to truly consider it. Ellie licked her lips, and her mouth felt dry.

"But we always cuddle." Louie's eyes rapidly scanned the air before him. His breathing quickened, and he looked at his hands. "I really thought you'd like this form. I screwed up."

There it was again. Ellie wrapped her arms around Louie and pulled him in close for a hug. "You're perfect."

"Then why won't you cuddle with me? You always told me how much you love me, my kisses, my cuddles. Now you're cringing at me." For the first time, she felt him shudder, and a sob escaped his lips. "You're rejecting me. My witch is rejecting me. What have I done?"

"No, no, it's not that you did anything wrong." She stroked his back like her mom did for her the day her caterpillar died.

"What if I'm a dog when we are behind closed doors, and when we're outside, I'm a human?"

"We talked about this; I just want you to be your own person."

"But you don't like me." He whimpered.

Ellie pulled back and guided his chin up so she could look at him. His eyes glistened, and heartbreak pulled at his lips. She wanted to patch everything together and bring back that smile. "I love you; that will never change."

Louie's eyebrows eased with her words.

"I just... you're a man now, right?"

Louie nodded.

Ellie searched the ceiling as she tried to find the right words. "And your reasoning for choosing a human was really good, really logical, and helpful."

He nodded with a little more enthusiasm.

"You created this 'form.'" She gestured with air quotation marks. "Using models from magazines that you saw I liked."

"I did." A proud smile crossed his face.

"Models are attractive people." She hoped he would connect the dots.

"Right."

Void help me.

She spoke slowly and deliberately. "So, you've made yourself into an attractive person."

"I tried." He continued to beam.

With an exhale and slumped shoulders, Ellie caved. "It makes me nervous."

Louie reeled his head back. "Nervous?"

"Yes, not the nervousness you'd feel being surrounded by bees, but nervous like you're going to jump off a waterfall."

He looked down as if he was calculating something. "I don't get it; both are dangerous."

"Maybe a hint of danger—but more like a fun, exciting adventure." She sat back on her feet.

"Okay." Louie sat thoughtfully. "Would it make you more comfortable if I looked like your dad or mom?"

"Oh, Void no!" Ellie took Louie's hand. "Please do not *ever* do that. This form, you, this, it's all fine. It is all great. It's just... it's a big change, and cuddling is so intimate." She grasped at straws. "It's just something I have to get used to."

Louie's head familiarly tilted to the side. The mannerisms he learned to adapt to as a dog would take time to leave. "How do we do that?"

"Well, maybe instead of you cuddling me, let me cuddle you?"

"You want to cuddle me?" He smiled sweetly.

Relief washed over her. "Well, for now, how about we just lie beside one another?"

"Oh! I could do that." Louie hurried over to her side of the bed and pulled the blankets back more for her. He moved quickly, excitedly, from side to side before he dropped like a stiff log on his back on one side of the bed with such force it made Ellie bounce.

"Spaz." She chuckled and returned to her side.

Side by side, she stared at the finished wooden ceiling above them. She couldn't help but notice that their arms touched.

"I see an owl," Louie broke the silence. "Look at the knots there."

Ellie followed his finger to the two knots of wood relatively close together. The way they were laid out, the ripples around them, it did kind of look like an owl. For her, it looked more like a crazed cat. He chuckled at her suggestion and pointed out another figure in the wood. As the awkwardness melted away, she was able to relax. Eventually, the familiar theme song of a television show got their attention, and Ellie drifted off to sleep to a rerun.

18

Cardinals

A creature of darkness, a disembodied voice beckoned her from a distance. *The Void calls.*

Ellie sat on the edge of the surf as waves rolled toward her. The sun neither rose nor set. It sat on the horizon, frozen in time. Hours passed, and it went unmoved.

"Where am I?" Her own words echoed through the space.

Suddenly, the perpetual darkness of night overshadowed the sun's bleeding colors. Somehow, Ellie could see as if it were midday, but there was no sun, no light to aid her.

Amongst the powerful, unending waves, a leathery, glistening head bobbed like a cork. A seal. This pinniped was unlike the one she saw on the beach. Instead of beady eyes above its black nose against a fat snout, its eyes shimmered with a silvery, hollow hue. It was eerie and made Ellie's heart thump in her chest.

Lost and alone.

The source of the disembodied voice made itself known as it wobbled from wave to wave menacingly.

Save them.

"But I'm not lost or alone," Ellie called out as if she could reason with this strange creature. "I have Louie. Who am I saving?"

She was met with faint, indiscernible whispers.

Shaking her head from side to side, Ellie had enough of this torment from the doomsday seal. "I'm outta here, creepy."

As she stood, the sand gave way under her feet. It was much deeper than earlier— and more viscous.

As she stumbled over her own foot, she shouted, "Are you kidding me?"

Quickly, the fine grains turned to liquid—a slow-moving, gooey liquid. As she tried to lift her hand, it felt heavy, and suddenly, she was being sucked into the sand. The world around her started to disappear as the ground slowly consumed her.

"Louie?" she cried out as she tried to crawl for the edge.

A crea-crea-crea-creature of dark-dark-dark-ness-ness, the disembodied voice echoed around the liquid crater.

As if summoned to the rescue, a happy little basset hound puppy ran toward her. A bell on its neck chimed away as it approached. "Louie!"

Ellie tried desperately to swim toward it, but the ground rose higher around her. Her limbs felt like they had cinder blocks tied to them.

El-El-El-lie-lie-lie-eee–Lynne-Lynne-Lynne

F-f-f-fate-fate-fate-fate

The puppy took a seat at the edge of the pool and curiously looked down at Ellie as she desperately reached for it.

"Louie, help me!"

It tilted its head from one side to the other. As it stared at her, the reality of the situation sank in.

Louie doesn't wear a bell. He doesn't have a brown splotch over his eye. "You're not Louie!"

That dog, her mother's voice boomed through the darkness as it grew around her and gobbled her up. This wasn't just a regular darkness like she'd find in the deep woods behind her parents' house in Connecticut. No, this was an oppressive darkness that hung in the air and carried into her lungs. She couldn't constrict her chest. The fear of suffocating engulfed her, and Ellie's heart beat so fast in her chest, she couldn't breathe.

Mmm, mmmm, a soothing tune slipped into her mind and drowned out all other thoughts. *Mmm, hmmm.*

A calming warmth filled her core and chased away the smothering feeling with every new note. The heat charged through her lungs like a mother grizzly bear, up her windpipe, and back out of her mouth. Relief and peace overcame her.

When Ellie woke, the sound of chickadees sang through the window outside. Her head rested against something wonderfully warm, and she heard the soft thump-thump of a heartbeat. Ellie opened her eyes and took in the sight before her. She had cuddled up to Louie in her sleep, with one leg draped over both of his, her head on his chest, and her arm around his stomach.

So intimate... Her own words rang through her head. *It's not okay for him to do it, but it's okay for you?*

But she still didn't move.

You're such a hypocrite. Ellie glanced up at his resting, peaceful face. Memories of it distorted with sadness made her hug him a little tighter. *Gods, you suck.*

With a sigh through her nose, Ellie pulled herself to sit upright. With hands over her face, Ellie groaned and rubbed her forehead.

How can you be attracted to your best friend? It's been twenty-four hours since he changed from a dog. You're treating his form flippantly, and you said you didn't want that! Ugh.

"Stop thinking about it," she whispered into her hands. "Occupy yourself; do something."

Determined to break the negative thoughts, Ellie made her way to the bathroom and took her first wonderful, hot shower in days. The luxury of warm water and floral scents occupied her senses. Her mind soon was at peace. By the time she emerged from the bathroom dressed for the day, Louie was awake. He stood in front of the small mirror mounted by the front door and looked at himself as he tested out different silly faces.

"What're you doing?" Ellie smirked.

"I have eyebrows now." Louie gave them a wiggle in the mirror. "They're so fun. Check this out." Louie lowered his left eyebrow and raised his right eyebrow. Then, he switched them. Back and forth, they bounced until his point was satisfied. "Eh?"

She loved how the little things were so amazing for him. "Alright, Eyebrow Man. You can keep that up, but I'm going to meditate."

"Oh! Let me join you." Even as a man, he still had puppy energy.

Ellie turned off the television, took a seat in the most open part of the floor, and crossed her legs. Louie took a seat beside her and mimicked her posture. Together, they shut their eyes and took a deep breath.

Unsurprisingly, thoughts of screaming at her mother before she left, the two men doubled over in Boston, the haunting prophecy, and her nightmare floated to the surface, but each time the thoughts interrupted her peace, she focused on her breath.

It took close to half an hour for Ellie to be able to find her center and feel a connection to the Void. When she emerged, Louie still had his eyes closed.

Weird, normally, he's done before me.

Respectfully, she gave him his time. She climbed into the chair by the window where she had taken her phone call with her father the night before and admired the scenery outside. Amongst the trees, she spotted a small bird feeder that looked like a metal cage filled with a block of seed. It wasn't just chickadees that graced her with their presence. A couple of squirrels and even a male cardinal scavenged along the grass.

Ellie adored the male cardinal's vibrant red plumage, taking up most of its body. Lowlights of jet black colored the tips of its wings and faded up its length. The funny little creature adorned a black mask around its eyes and under its chin. Typically, Ellie and Louie would search for the female bird together.

The sound of the tiny, four-cup glass carafe clinked, pulling Ellie's attention away from the scenery outside. Louie stood at the small, one-basin sink, filling the coffee pot. A wide smile crossed her lips as she remembered his attempt to give her breakfast in bed on her sixteenth birthday. A circular wicker basket with a large handle contained a chocolate chip banana oatmeal muffin, a travel mug filled with coffee, and a chopped apple in an old mug.

"No muffins and apples?"

"Unfortunately, not this morning." Louie offered her a smile as he loaded up the coffee maker like Elijah had done many Saturdays before. "I did see those little hard cookies you like in a vending machine."

"I don't need cookies for breakfast."

"Sounds like a good breakfast to me," he said with a shrug.

The smell of freshly brewed coffee soon filled the little cabin. Louie and Ellie sat at the window and sipped at their respective cups while they observed the birds. Of course, he spotted the female cardinal in seconds.

"Did you know they mate for life?" Ellie shared. "The male watches over the female while she eats."

"Oh yes, you've told me," he added politely.

After check-out, with renewed energy and hope, the indomitable duo continued their journey of discovery, freedom, and adventure. The main road took them through more small towns, past swamps, lakes, and a never-ending line of trees.

Provincetown, the quirky, colorful seaside community, greeted them that late morning with seagulls, a partially cloudy sky, and a few tourists. Memorial Day weekend had just passed, and according to the owner of the Northern Sea Star Cafe, the tourists would overtake the shops soon. Ellie quickly learned Cape Cod was one area that survived on the generous contributions of travelers.

Commercial Street, the main street, was populated by tightly tucked-together businesses. Grease from the restaurants and the smell of the ocean hung in the air as Louie and Ellie walked down the brick sidewalks. Pristine white park benches sat along cement walls that held back beautiful gardens or supported tourist-oriented businesses. It seemed like every livable, non-business-oriented place they passed had small apartments on the second floor with no yards, only balconies.

"I like that one." Ellie pointed out a small balcony off the side of a building above a novelty shop.

"You couldn't have a garden in a place like this, though," Louie reminded her. "A witch needs a garden."

Eventually, they found their way to a book shop tucked between a brick Post Office and an overly decorated ice cream shop, complete with pink and blue swirls and a massive wooden soft ice cream cone protruding into the street, as well as a happy cow painted on the window.

Ellie read the sign aloud, "Turn of the Page—Bookstore and Art Supplies."

The bookstore was extensive for such a small area. Three large display windows showed their wares—canvasses, a beautiful gray yarn blanket draped over a wooden chair, and a foam pumpkin with artist carving tools shoved into the top of it. Ellie also saw best-seller books, novels from local authors, and a bed for a large dog.

"This place looks amazing. Let's check it out," Ellie declared.

Inside, the store was beautifully set up with alternating art supplies and book displays. Suede black couches and matching armchairs were perfectly set up beside end tables and a fake fireplace. A single-cup coffee maker sat beside the fake fireplace with an assortment of coffees and teas to choose from, with a sign that read, "$1 per cup."

"I love this place," Ellie announced as they passed by the machine. Bean bag chairs and house plants added to the welcoming display of the surprising two-floor store.

The second floor had a broader array of books. A section dedicated to herbalism, tarot cards, and crystals took up an entire corner, filled with bright colors and drapery. She was about to explore that section when a mass of curly, strawberry-blond hair popped up from behind one of the bookshelves next to it. The curls belonged to a short woman with slender cheeks, a beautiful smile, and kind eyes covered by glasses.

"Oh!" She jumped back, clutching the book in her hand over her heart.

"Ah!" Ellie backed into Louie, who caught her before she could run into a bookshelf.

Together, the two women gained their senses and laughed.

"Oh, you two." As she flipped her hand in the air, her many bracelets jingled. Everything about her attire was flowy. "You scared me."

"Sorry. I saw the tarot cards and got excited."

"They have a new set." As she held up her pack, her eyes seemed distracted by something above Ellie and Louie's heads. A quizzical look crossed her face. "Do you do readings?"

"Oh, no." Ellie chuckled, then looked at Louie and above his head. "I just like the art."

"Me too." Her eyes studied them for a moment. "Forgive me. This may seem weird, but you two are new here, right?"

Ellie awkwardly shifted her weight. "Yeah. We just got in yesterday."

"Are you and your Familiar visiting family?"

19

Luna

O h, sorry to put you on the spot like this. I should introduce myself." The woman in the bohemian-looking dress extended a fabulously manicured hand with shimmering jewels on their tips. "I'm Luna."

It took Ellie a moment to register the introduction. "Familiar... you know he's... how?"

Luna looked around the room cautiously, then leaned in. "I can see your connection to the Void; that's my gift." She winked as she straightened up.

Ellie smiled awkwardly and brought her hands together in front of her. "I'm Ellie." She gestured to her side. "This is Louie."

Louie leaned around Ellie and extended his hand to Luna. Her bracelets jingled, and she braced an arm over her dress as he greeted her.

"Aren't you friendly?" She laughed and readjusted herself the moment he let go. "I'd be a terrible local if I didn't offer to show you around—or a cup of coffee. I live just around the corner if I can tempt you?"

Ellie turned to Louie, who could spot a bee from a mile away. He didn't look worried or guarded. Ellie took in Luna's attire a second time, and nothing matched her father's warning or description of people to avoid.

"Yeah, sure!"

The trio headed down the stairs and past the still-life display.

"Nothing today, Luna?" the young woman with green reading glasses around her neck called out from behind the counter.

"I may be back later," Luna called back. "Have a good one."

"See you then."

Luna led Ellie and Louie down a couple of blocks into the residential side of town. Here, the houses were squished close to one another with little yard space between them.

Ugh, I could reach an arm out and be in their living room.

Luna's brick bungalow sat back from the sidewalk. A white picket fence with small matching towers made a division between her yard and the sidewalk. Beautiful purple and pink flowers burst out from the fence, threatening to brush against any exposed calves that passed. The lively yard was divided by a stone walking path that led to a covered porch. A little driveway ran along the right side of the house, and a brick wall closed it off from the neighbors. Between the house and the garage, a pergola with vines along it added a pop of green to the space. The familiar sound of thick nails clacked against the hard tiles inside the house as Luna opened the door into the quaint kitchen. A fluffy, small, red Pomeranian with a white underbelly greeted the group.

"Mitsy! We have guests. Say hello." Luna hung her keys on a wall-mounted hook by the door and kicked off her sandals.

Mitsy sniffed Ellie and Louie before she spun in a circle, emitting a small puff of red fur that hung in the air.

"Sorry, she's always shedding."

"Is she your Familiar?" Ellie asked before she cautiously knelt down to give the puffball a pat.

"No, just my dear friend." Luna went to the coffee station on the small counter and began to fix them a fresh pot.

The house was small but beautiful.

"Get comfy out on the patio. Mitsy will lead you." Luna directed them down the hallway. "I'll be out in a moment."

Mitsy happily led them down the hallway, her head held high. She stopped at the back door and hopped up with extended front paws.

"I know that feeling, buddy." Louie leaned around and opened the door for them.

"Show off," Ellie teased.

The backyard was small, but Luna used every inch of space. The walls had planter boxes and lattice for all types of plants Ellie recognized. A cute little workstation was set up in the corner with a small overhang and a tiny stool. It all looked well thought out, but also natural and overgrown.

"This place is going to be gorgeous in late June," Ellie commented to Louie as they took their seats on a porch swing loaded with pillows. A comfy wicker chair sat across from them with a large pillow, a matching footrest, and a side table. Luna stepped outside with steaming cups of coffee accompanied by a carafe for refills, milk, and sugar.

She set down the tray and passed out cups before she took her seat. Mitsy climbed into her lap. From her pocket, she pulled out a bone-shaped treat, broke it into manageable pieces, and passed the first bite to Mitsy.

"So yeah, welcome to Provincetown." Luna chuckled. "What brings you two here?"

"We're kind of on a road trip." Now that it left her lips, it felt lame.

"How fun! I love road trips. Where are you from? Where've you been?"

"We're from a little town in Connecticut. Are you familiar with the Frog Pond Reserve?"

Luna shook her head.

"Well, that's okay, not important. We went to Boston and then here." Ellie pointed to an imaginary map that floated before her.

"What did you think of the city?"

Ellie didn't hold back. Once she ripped off the Band-Aid about her hatred for the city, she told Luna everything, including Louie's shift.

"Wow! So, you just shifted?"

Louie nodded sheepishly.

"Like, *just* shifted?" Luna asked.

He nodded again, then looked at Ellie.

"First time?"

"Yes," Ellie answered.

"That's such a huge change! I've spoken with friends and friends of friends who have gone through this transition. How are you two handling it?"

"We uh... wait—others? Does this happen a lot?"

"Oh yeah, and it can be a big change! For some, it's no big deal. It's like every time I see them, their Familiar has changed. A cat, a dog, a raccoon, so many things."

Luna swatted at a fly, and Mitsy broke from her munching to let out a growl. Luna took a moment to work through her thoughts and get back to her point.

"For others, like you, where their Familiar has always had just one form, it's been a staple, a comfort blanket for so long, it can be a jarring change, like splashing ice water over yourself."

Jarring—that word hits the nail on the head. Ellie crossed one leg over the other and leaned forward. "It's been... difficult," Ellie admitted. "Not in a negative way. It's just been a lot."

Ellie noticed Louie shift beside her.

"Did you two have any time to talk between the change and coming here?"

Ellie sheepishly looked at Louie as she thought of her breakdown on the beach and the talk in the cabin. "A little bit, yeah."

"And?" Luna took another sip. "Sorry if I just dive right into it. I worked in mental health for decades. The complications of transition, being that vulnerable and raw, are my bread and butter. I could talk about it all day."

As Luna expressed apologies, Louie's finger gently brushed against the small bulge in Ellie's pocket. Ellie's eyebrows furrowed with confusion, and then she remembered her shell and that incredible hug. When Ellie looked back, Luna had a tight-lipped, coy smile on her face.

"Decades?" Ellie tried to take the attention off them. "How old are you?"

"Fifty-four."

She reeled back. "What? How? You look so young."

"Oh, you're sweet." Luna waved off the compliment. "Thank you."

Although small talk was nice, Ellie only knew of one person, her ancestor Ahren Wagner, who had a Familiar. "What else can you tell me about Familiars?"

Luna looked to Louie and then to her. "What do you want to know?"

"Everything."

Luna's green eyes looked up to the ceiling, like she chased a thought. "It sounds like you don't know much about them?"

Ellie shook her head from side to side.

"Where'd you say you went to school?"

"I was homeschooled from twelve up," Ellie told her.

"And you're from Connecticut." Luna's words were slower now, like she had put something together.

"Yes."

"Northern Connecticut? Like near the Mass border? Bridgwater area?"

Ellie thought back to the surrounding towns. After a moment, she nodded.

"Alright, why don't you tell me what you know, and I can fill in the spaces from there?"

Ellie looked at Louie who poured most of the contents of the milk container into his cup. "You want to tell her?" Ellie gently nudged him.

Louie looked down at his freshly made cup of coffee, then up to Ellie and Luna. "Yeah, I can. It was the new moon, the month before Ellie's birth."

Ellie leaned back in her chair and watched him as he retold their story.

"...the two of us walked until we found the pool that led to Ellie. And, well, when it was my time to go down, Seer kicked me in the butt, and I landed in the cake."

Luna closed her eyes and slowly opened them. "What's this about a cake?"

Ellie took over and told her all about the Becoming Ceremony, Mee-Maw's terrible cake, and Louie crashing down.

"That is an enchanting story. Anything else?"

"Just that the last member of my family to have a Familiar was Ahren Wagner."

Luna sputtered into her coffee, spilling the contents of her cup onto her dress and chest. "Oh no! I love this dress. Up, up, Mitsy-Boo."

Mitsy hopped off Luna's lap onto the floor.

"Pardon me. I need to change and treat this stain quickly."

Luna fluttered off into the house. From the porch, they heard doors open and close inside.

"What was that about?" Ellie asked Louie.

"I don't know."

"Well, I hope she saves her dress."

Louie chugged down his mixture of milk and a little bit of coffee. He placed his cup on the side table and caught the eyes of the red and white puffball. "Hi there!"

Mitsy happily yipped at him. When Luna returned to the porch, she found Louie on his back, with Mitsy contentedly settled on his chest as she licked his face.

"Mitsy-Boo, you made a new friend."

"She's very sweet."

Luna was now dressed in a beautiful V-neck, short sleeve, A-line dress that accentuated her frame. The dark colors beautifully popped against her sun-kissed skin.

"I was thinking about what you shared with me, regarding your knowledge on Familiars. You know, down in Eastham, it's like the hub of our little magical community. We have a library with classes anybody with membership can attend."

Luna grabbed a fresh cup of coffee and returned to her chair, so Mitsy abandoned Louie to return to her favorite seat.

"You could really get a full circle there. I don't want to do you a disservice by robbing you of information."

A class? I haven't been in a classroom since the seventh grade. Ellie's humiliating last day of school, when she developed her mark, played through her mind.

"How young would my classmates be?" Ellie asked. The idea of being in class with twelve-year-olds didn't feel appealing to her.

"Oh, all ages. It's not like a first-grade, second-grade sort of setup. It's typically pre-teens up." A sweet giggle left her lips. "At my age, everybody is a youngster."

Ellie's shoulders relaxed. That really didn't sound so bad. It actually sounded fun. "Could Louie come?"

"Of course! Familiars are always welcome to any event, venue... anything."

"Really? Anything?" She looked up to Louie.

"Oh yes, everything," Luna clarified.

"No red bowls," Louie said with a smirk.

They stayed and spoke with Luna until mid-afternoon. When they finally wrapped up their chat, she escorted them back to the bookstore.

"Before you go." Luna turned on her heels. "We do a monthly celebration here—a New Moon Party, if you will. Would you two like to join us?"

"A party?" Louie bounced on his toes.

"Oh yes, lots of witches, wizards, Familiars. Would you two like to join?"

A real party!

"No pressure." Luna pulled out a notepad from her purse and quickly jotted down a note on a blank page before she ripped it out and handed it to Ellie. "If you come, you come! My number's on the bottom if you get lost. Things really get rolling after sunset. I hope to see you both there."

Mitsy gave them a happy yip from under Luna's arm before she walked away with a little wave goodbye.

They were a couple of doors down before Ellie burst with excitement. "We got invited to a party!"

Louie joined in her excited hop.

"What do we wear? I can't wear these old clothes. Do we need to bring something? Mom always said it was rude not to bring something. What do we bring?" Ellie asked.

While they brainstormed and fantasized about the party, they stumbled across a large restaurant on a main corner. Just as Mary had explained, The Shell Pile was right before the old wooden pier.

"Ellie!" Louie excitedly pulled her hand as they rushed down the brick sidewalk to the sandy beach that extended under the pier.

Old, water-damaged beams held up the massive structure above their head. The tide was out, and moist, hard sand occupied the area. The shadows of the buildings, the beams, and the dock covered most of the soil below their feet. The ground was littered with rocks, broken shells, and full, gorgeous, light-brown spiral shells that slowly scurried along.

"Look!"

Ellie and Louie knelt amongst the wet sand and watched. From the front of the shells, they saw four fat legs, small little back legs, silly elongated antennae, fat claws, and stalked eyes. There were dozens of them!

"Look at this one... and this one," Ellie pointed out excitedly to Louie.

"Oh!" Louie stepped away for a moment.

"Hurry up, you're missing it."

"I'm here. I'm here." Louie popped up next to her with an empty, beautiful spiral shell in hand. It was larger than the other shells on the ground.

Thoughtfully, he placed it next to the largest crab. Much to Louie's pleasure, the hermit crab walked over to inspect his offering. Seemingly happy with the condition of the new shell, it slipped from its old home into its new one. Others followed along, trading off shell for shell.

"Oh my god! Look what you've done!" Ellie laughed. "You've disrupted the free market."

Ellie and Louie watched the show for half an hour before they moved along.

Before they left Provincetown, Ellie and Louie stopped by a small grocery store and gathered some provisions for the night: a bag of oranges, water, and fixings for peanut butter and jelly sandwiches.

With the New Moon Party just a night away, Ellie decided to drive back down to Eastham and find a camping place within the vicinity. Tonight, they would sleep under the night sky in a tent. Ellie couldn't justify another night of luxury in a hotel since they were still at the beginning of their journey. With some guidance from a free tourist brochure, she located Fort Hill Overlook. It was a gorgeous, flat meadow that looked out over the cove.

Ellie and Louie found a private spot in the woods, secluded from the hiking trail and prying eyes, to set up their tent for the night. Here, they didn't have to worry about police with flashlights or an unstable woman who threw bottles—and they couldn't hear cars, trucks, or eighteen-wheelers. Here, the wind whistled through the trees, and the water rumbled against the shore off in the distance.

Louie and Ellie set up the tent and their dinner before it got dark. While they sat in the tent, Louie peeled the oranges, and Ellie made sandwiches, but her mind whirred with the intensity of their journey. Suddenly, a though popped into her head.

One spring eve. Ellie shuddered at the thought.

"What's up, butter cup?"

"Just a lot on my mind," she admitted and popped a juicy slice of orange into her mouth.

"I think I know something that could help with that." Louie ushered Ellie out of the tent.

Dressed in her pajamas, Ellie followed Louie into the woods and down towards the cove. Out here, away from the city, they could once again see the night sky above. Ellie was surprised that Louie had removed the blanket from the backpack without her knowledge and laid it out in the grass.

"What's this?" Ellie exclaimed excitedly.

"I thought we could just be. Like back in the orchard."

If it was anybody other than Louie who laid out a blanket for her in the middle of a beautiful meadow beneath the night sky, she would have suspicions about their motives, but not Louie. She climbed onto the blanket and lay beside him.

Above them, a sea of stars sparkled. For Ellie, that meant a story book of old tales. Louie extended a finger and pointed to a constellation in the southern portion of the sky. "What's that?"

"Virgo." Ellie smiled because he already knew the answer.

"Story?" Louie asked hopefully.

With a soft expression, Ellie happily retold the tale. "Virgo comes from Greek mythology." She turned to lay on her side. Ellie's arm supported her head, and her free hand traced the shape of the constellation. "It was spring when Hades kidnapped Persephone. She was the daughter of the Earth goddess, Demeter. Her mother was overcome with grief by the loss of her daughter and abandoned her responsibilities. So, fertility and fruitfulness suffered—"

"That means the plants withered up, right?"

"Right." Ellie smirked. *You always ask that.* It didn't break her stride. "So, Zeus got involved in everything and demanded Hades allow Persephone to return to her mother. A condition of this return was that Persephone wasn't allowed to eat until her return. To sabotage this, Hades gave Persephone a pomegranate to eat."

Louie dramatically gasped.

"Because of that, Persephone must return to the Underworld for four months every year, and that's why when her constellation is missing from the sky, we have winter."

Louie had the sweetest smile on his face. His eyes searched the night sky. "That one?"

"Which one?" Ellie leaned in and pressed her head against his hand. She followed the line his finger made. "Oh, Cronus!"

They lay there for a couple of hours as she retold the stories about the constellations and the myths behind them. When Ellie grew tired enough, they packed up the blanket. Louie shook it out to get rid of the ticks, gave Ellie a once over to make sure she hadn't gained any creepy crawly stowaways, and accompanied Ellie back to the tent.

She climbed into the sleeping bag on top of the thin sleeping mat. Ellie closed her eyes, took a deep breath in through her nose, and stretched. When she opened her eyes, Louie lay on his side outside of the sleeping bag, off of the mat on the cold, hard ground.

You've kicked him out of the bed like he's some creep, some stranger. When he was a basset hound, Louie would wiggle his way in and lay on top of her. They would be two snuggly peas in a pod. Now, if she didn't let him in the sleeping bag, he truly would be like a second-class citizen.

Ellie swallowed hard. "Hey."

Louie turned to look at her. He didn't look bothered by the current arrangement.

"Come here."

20

Invitation

A *creature of darkness.*

Beads of sweat coated her forehead as Ellie lay in the sleeping bag. Thinking of the sea of stars above, filled with magical, ancient stories of love, betrayal, grief, and war, distracted her from sleep.

If I only had to deal with goatfish and horny, narcissistic thunder-gods, this would be so much easier. With a weary sigh, she ran her free hand through her hair. *Creatures of darkness... living in darkness or made from darkness? That could be the depths of the ocean, their moral compass, or what they are made of. Couldn't have been more direct, could you, Betty?* Ellie's stomach churned into a knot. *The library would have been a great place to decipher this. Mom probably has an entire handwritten journal with lists of dark creatures.*

Minutes turned into hours as she tried to remember every obscure creature her mother taught her about. Unfortunately, their exploration into creatures of malicious intent was limited.

I can see why; she probably didn't want to think about it.

The list went from magical and mythical to normal creatures living in caves and forests. Her mental shake-down went on until birds began to sing just before dawn. Meanwhile, Louie slept like a baby in her arms. His head lay on her shoulder, his blond hair tickling her face.

I could learn more about you. She leaned into his head. *You could learn to read. We could maybe even meet others with Familiars.* Her fingertips danced through his hair. *How could Mom and Dad not know about a place like this? A school, a big community. They only ever spoke of Oren. This place is only a couple of hours away. It just doesn't add up.*

She ruminated over her childhood education, her final days in public school, and the day she received her mark, which eventually lulled her back to sleep.

"I woke up before you. I woke up before you." The chanting of Louie's voice broke through her dreamless sleep.

Ellie was trapped inside the blanket cocoon, unable to get away. Before her eyes could open, she felt the scritchy-scratchy feel of rough hair against her shoulder and neck.

His beard.

"I get to annoy you," Louie continued to sing-song as he tickled and nudged her with his head.

"Ugh!" Even as a human, he still used his head like a battering ram for this morning ritual. Ellie tensed. "No, no, I want to sl—"

A warm, wet tongue pressed against the bottom of her chin and dragged up the length of her cheek. Ellie's mouth dropped open wide in shock as she was forced wide awake.

"You jerk! That's so gross."

Louie let out an evil snicker. "I get to annoy you."

"Oh, I'll show you annoying!"

The most charming wrestling match ensued in the purple and gray tent. Laughter filled the air around, drowning out the sound of the early morning songbirds. For the first time in a long time, Ellie welcomed the day with joy.

The cove and meadow provided ample entertainment in the form of seabirds, gorgeous wildflowers, and creatures that dwelled beneath the wet sands of the surf. They occupied their day by foraging for food, eating lunch, and shopping at a small thrift store they passed the day before in Eastham.

"I can't wear these dirty clothes to our first party," she explained as she went through the clothes on the circular metal rack.

"You'll smell like Mee-Maw's house in these clothes, though."

Louie had a point—the smell of potpourri permeated everything in the store.

"You win some, you lose some?" She shrugged with an unconvincing smile.

A small changing room tucked away in the far back corner provided Ellie privacy.

As she dressed for the party, she couldn't help but remember the first time she was invited to a birthday party. The invitation was not much larger than an index card and was given under the promise of secrecy on the playground.

"Not everyone is invited," Mindy had whispered underneath the slide.

Ellie had immediately tucked the invitation into the pocket of her overalls. After recess ended and the children were called back inside for more times tables, Ellie politely excused herself to use the restroom. Between the bright-red bathroom stalls, she stood in front of the toilet in isolation and pulled out the invitation. Ellie was excited since Mindy had promised streamers, a pool, her basset hound, Mr. Peanut, and a piñata.

"No," Kimberly had said and tossed the invitation onto the kitchen counter. "I'm sorry, Ellie. We have plans that day."

"But it's her birthday. Please?"

"I said no. Go do your homework."

After that, Ellie concluded that birthdays were just one more "normal" thing her mother wouldn't let her do.

Now, on the last day of May, Ellie was actually preparing to go to a party. She stood before an old mirror in a baggy purple sweater and jeans.

"I think I'm going to wear them out," she called to Louie on the other side of the door.

***

The address Luna provided led them to a driveway with a smiley-face balloon mounted to the mailbox.

"Bop!" Louie excitedly hit it. The foil crinkled under his fist, and the smile shimmered. "Nervous?"

Ellie nodded. The turnout was much more than she had expected. Maybe five, six witches and wizards. But this? The driveway was full. Cars were parked along the rural stretch of road on both sides. Their motorcycle sat far down the line, near the neighbor's house.

I'm going to look like an idiot. The idea of turning around and running back to their campsite crossed her mind.

"You?"

"Not at all." Louie offered Ellie his elbow.

"Really?" She accepted it.

"Yeah." He confidently stepped forward. "Because... It's just," Louie began the start of a familiar song they made up together. "Me and Lou. You and me."

"Just the two of us," Ellie added.

"Louie and Ellie," they chimed in together.

"Just me with Lou." She leaned into his arm.

"And me with E." Louie swayed back into her.

"Just the two of us. The world will see!"

"Think they'll like us?" Louie asked.

"Eh, if they don't, I like you enough for all of them." Ellie nudged him.

The house was not visible from the road, but after ten feet, it peered out from around large, lush hedges. It was a grand, luxurious waterfront property. If Ellie were to compare it to the bungalow from yesterday, the detached garage alone would be about twice the size of it.

A large, wooden porch stretched the length of the front of the house, and twinkling white lights wrapped around the railings. People with cigarettes dangling from their fingers populated the area.

As Ellie and Louie walked up the steps, she couldn't help but feel eyes on them. Her instinct was to look up, smile, and say, "Hi," but after Boston, she wasn't so sure.

"Hey!" The greeting was loud enough to pull Ellie out of her shy bubble. A young woman with a cigarette between her fingers offered her a smile.

"Hi." Louie offered an enthusiastic wave. It was endearing but embarrassing.

Ellie laughed, grabbed his hand, and pulled it down. "Come on." She pulled him inside.

While the number of cars would suggest a rager, it was wonderfully peaceful inside. Parents sat in the living room and watched a kid's movie while small children played on the floor with toys. The largest concentration of people was in the stylish kitchen. The moment Ellie saw a plate of food, she nudged Louie. "Check it out."

Like vultures, Ellie and Louie descended upon the hors d'oeuvres: little oval pieces of toasted bread had some sort of spread and grape-like things on it; fanned pastry cups with some sort of soft cheese, bits of chives, and maybe dried red peppers; squishy, short, white cylinders wrapped with bacon; a cherry tomato, leaf of fresh basil, and mozzarella on little toothpicks and drizzled with olive oil; mini hotdogs wrapped in a crust; upside-down mushrooms stuffed with a mixture; and oysters.

A wicked smile crossed Ellie's lips as she held up the tiny mound of meat in a chilled shell. "Dare you."

Without hesitation, Louie leaned forward and took the entire thing into his mouth.

Ellie's eyes opened wide. "You're not supposed to eat the—"

He paused mid-bite and shifted the contents of his mouth around. "Hm."

To her horror, Louie's eyebrows furrowed.

"Are you okay?" Ellie could only imagine the cuts in his mouth at this point. *Oh gods, did I just kill my Familiar with an appetizer?*

Those hair-covered cheeks glowed like a warm candle. Ellie had seen Louie exterminate bees once before, and this reminded her of exactly that.

"Interesting," Louie said thoughtfully.

"What do you mean interesting?" Ellie exclaimed.

"First time with shellfish?" A young man with jet-black hair, well-defined cheekbones, and a slender nose coolly stepped up next to Louie. He was dressed stylishly in a gray blazer, matching slacks, and shiny shoes. A martini glass carefully sat in his hand with a single small, white olive on a toothpick inside the clouded liquid.

"Mhm." Louie nodded.

The stranger leaned in as if he was about to share a trade secret. "Same thing happened to me. Always remove it from the shell, or it freaks out the humans."

The man turned to look at Ellie and gave her a respectful head nod before he disappeared back into the crowd. Awkwardly, Ellie returned the nod before she stepped back in close to Louie.

"Was that another Familiar?" she whispered.

"Yeah!" Louie said in awe.

Their mutual admiration for the good-looking, well-dressed Familiar was interrupted by a little yip. Louie looked down, and a grin spread widely across his face. A friendly Pomeranian sat by their feet.

"Look who it is! Hello, dear friend," Louie greeted her.

Ellie took Louie's plate from him so he could pick up the affectionate pup, who assaulted his face with kisses. The gentle lights from the porch on the other side of the window lit up his face.

Admiring him, Ellie thought, *Louie doesn't need fancy clothes to look good.*

"Hey, Mitsy." Ellie gently scratched the angelic dog behind the ear, but it did nothing. Mitsy nuzzled into Louie's shoulder. Any time he tried to put her down, she threw a fit and began to howl.

"Guess that decision's made for you." Ellie nodded towards the back porch. "Let's find a place to sit and eat."

Louie opened the sliding glass door before her, and Ellie carried their food outside onto the wooden deck. It was covered and had a large grill at the far-left-hand side, which was populated by some boisterous men with beers and tongs. The smell of hot dogs filled the air. *Who'd want hotdogs when they could have any of this?*

The stairs descended a small hill into beach sand. Children played with glow-in-the-dark toys and sparklers as the last few moments of dusk blessed them.

"Louie, look!" On a bench carved from a driftwood tree, Mary from the Sugar Shack sat beside a young man with a hat and work-out clothes. Before them were a couple of kids—one dark-skinned pre-teen girl bounced a glow-in-the-dark soccer ball off her forehead while another girl, maybe a couple of years older than her, bounced a plain one off her knee.

"You called it." Louie nudged Ellie with his elbow.

A small series of short whistles sang through the air. "Mitsy-boo."

Arf, Mitsy called out next to Louie's ear.

He copied her, and the dog reeled her head back in surprise.

"Mits-Ah!" Luna excitedly hurried over to them. "You made it!"

She had a tall flute glass in hand, and bubbles danced to the top of the drink. Louie attempted to put Mitsy back down, but she howled again.

"Mits—let the boy be!" Luna took Mitsy from Louie, holding her like a baby over her shoulder. "How was the ride over? I hope it wasn't too much trouble finding the place."

"Not at all." Louie took back his plate. "The balloon made it easy."

"Oh, good." Ellie noticed a little twinkle in Luna's eye and the pink in her cheeks. "I have to admit; I was a little skeptical that you'd show up, but I'm so glad you did. This is such a great turn out. I mean, we always have a good turnout, but this is probably one of the bigger parties we've had in months. That's kind of par-for-the-course because of winter. So many people come and go with the season."

"I've never been to a party this big." *Don't rat me out, Lou.* "Is everyone here a witch or wizard?"

"Mostly." Luna thought for a moment. "Or spouses of witches and wizards. Familiars, too."

"Yeah, I think we just met one."

Ellie pointed back over her shoulder to the house and looked to Louie for help. Luna burst out laughing, and Ellie could see why. Louie had his cheeks completely stuffed and half of his plate empty. *Leave you alone for one moment, and you channel a chipmunk.*

"A Familiar, that is, um, tall, black hair—"

"Cheekbones you could cut an apple with?" Luna added.

"Yes!"

"That's Katie's Familiar, Jackson. They came from Jersey a few years ago, but now they live in this gorgeous beach house in Sandwich, tons of land. He had already shifted into this form by the time they arrived."

Luna stood on her toes for a moment as she looked around the crowd. Finally, she found them.

Katie and Jackson looked more like a couple than anything. Katie, a beautiful young woman with long, straight, blond hair pulled into an updo, wore a gorgeous evening gown that shimmered in the porch lights and accentuated her curves. Jackson's arm wrapped around Katie's waist and held her close.

"She's very fashionable," Luna commented.

"Yeah." The way they stood, with his hand around her, they definitely looked like a couple. *I've never stood like that with Louie.* Ellie swallowed hard. Katie and Jackson looked good together, and it seemed comfortable and acceptable to those around them, but it was such an intimate pose. "Are they," Ellie's voice grew small. "Together?"

"Oh yes." Luna smiled widely. "A few others here, too."

21

Pleasantries

Y ou know, some take that plunge."

Ellie almost choked when Luna said, "Plunge."

"Others decide not to. That's one of those things you'd learn about in those classes—" Luna broke off to give a polite smile and wave to an older gentleman who passed. She seemed to know everybody. "The bond between a person and their Familiar."

Bond? I don't need to sit through a lecture about our bond. I live the bond. Luna had continued to speak, but her back was to Ellie, and she had trailed off.

"What?" Ellie asked.

"I said, 'It's not every day you learn that you have—'"

"Luna! I've been looking everywhere for you." A man, who couldn't have been older than thirty-five with styled, combed-back hair and a five o'clock shadow, which only further accentuated his strong jaw line, hugged Luna tight.

Her head only just met the middle of his chest. He was well-groomed and very muscular. His shirt drew extra attention to the circumference of his biceps. A beautiful, ragdoll cat with blue eyes that put Ellie's to shame wrapped its elegant tail around his calf before it sat on his foot.

"Terry! Oh, it's so good to see you!" Luna greeted him.

The two old friends continued to talk.

Ellie couldn't take her eyes off the cat, who perched herself perfectly on Terry's foot. The cat had long, cream-colored fur that darkened to a burnt brown at the tip of its ears, tail, and paws. Its chest and nose were the lightest shade of cream out of its entire body.

"What?" It spoke in a very candid, soft voice.

Ellie jumped back in surprise. It didn't flinch. "You're very pretty."

The Familiar turned its attention to Louie. They shared a silent moment before it looked away.

"Susan." The man patted his shoulder, and the cat hopped up to it. "Would you like to say hi to Mitsy?"

"No." The cat thoughtfully adjusted a tuff of Terry's hair.

"I really would like to introduce my new friend, Ellie, to the Browns." Luna gave Terry's hand a gentle squeeze. "I'll stop by the shop next week?"

"You better. Those earrings won't stay long."

As soon as they were out of earshot, Ellie leaned in toward Luna. "They aren't? Are they?"

"Aren't what?"

"You know..." Ellie raised her eyebrows to drive home her point.

"Oh!" Luna almost jumped out of her skin at the thought of it. "No! Heavens no. Soulmate means something different to everybody."

Ellie stopped walking, and Louie caught her plate before the contents could spill onto the beach. "What? What now?"

"What?" Luna tilted her head.

"You said 'soulmate.'" Ellie cleared her tightening throat.

"I did? Oh yeah." Luna chuckled. "Familiars are soulmates, and soulmate means something different to different people."

Ellie hung on to her every word. It took all her willpower to not shake the answers out of Luna. "Go on."

"Well, for some, a soulmate is a friend they hold onto for life. For others, it's a pet, and for some, it's a lover." The jingle of her bracelets filled the air. "Everybody's different."

A soulmate? Louie stood beside her and seemed more interested in the bits of food on his plate than this information.

"I know the Wagner family believes Familiars are servants, but that's never been the truth." Luna beckoned them forward. "Come on. I have some friends I want you to meet."

A sea of faces passed Ellie as Luna introduced them. She couldn't focus on names and pleasantries. *Soulmates.* Her heart felt lighter, and her shoulders relaxed. *After everything, all the confusion, and this new form, I'm not some sort of freak. This makes so much sense.*

"...I am just so glad you came tonight!" The older woman with smile wrinkles and silver hair offered Ellie a well-practiced smile. The light of the fire illuminated her formal white suit and high-water pants beautifully.

"Thank you."

Ellie played along but never got the woman's name.

My best friend is my soulmate...

Luna led them over to the chairs surrounding the fire. A beautiful, colorful scarf was tied to the armrest of the seat, and Luna pulled it off. The moment she sat down and set Mitsy on her lap, the little dog hopped off and returned to Louie's ankles.

"You can sit here." A kind woman's voice one chair away danced through the air. The blue, child-sized, wind-suit jacket that occupied the seat between Luna and this stranger was removed.

"Oh, thanks." Ellie hadn't touched much of the food on her plate since they reached the beach. "You want to sit, Louie?"

"No, you sit. I can sit in front of you."

"Are you sure?"

"Yeah. I have a friend to entertain." He pointed down to the needy cotton ball. "You need to eat."

Always a gentleman. That flutter in her stomach was present again.

Ellie took the seat offered to her, and Louie sat at her feet. The sky had grown completely dark through the wave of introductions, and stars now twinkled above in the moonless sky.

In the center of the seats, the fire crackled and roared, offering warmth to everyone around it. Ellie knew she must have been introduced to every face lit by the orange glow, but she didn't remember a single name.

"Holy crap."

The most delicious meatball Ellie had ever eaten intruded on her mouth and thoughts.

"What?" Louie asked.

"Try this." Ellie held the other half of the meatball in front of Louie's face. He took the toothpick from her fingers before he tossed it into the fire.

"Oh, wow! That's good." He proceeded to hold up Mitsy, who happily cleaned the sauce from his facial hair.

"You two are cute." The woman who moved the jacket so Ellie could sit down spoke.

"Oh, thanks." The compelling urge to explain who Louie was to her ran to the front of her mind, but she stopped herself. *If I say he's my Familiar, is she going to assume we're together?* "He-uh, we..."

"You're from Connecticut, right?" The stranger took a swig from her amber bottle. "Sorry, Cape Cod is a big-small town."

"Yeah." Ellie was grateful for the change in subject.

"Which part? City? Country? North, south, east, west?" She had short-cut, salt and pepper hair that was squished down and mostly covered by a knitted beanie cap. Creases at the corner of her eyes in this terrible light gave away her age. She had to be in her late forties, maybe early fifties. She was thin and wore jeans and a long-sleeved, light-colored cotton shirt with a dark, puffy vest over it.

She looks oddly familiar.

"Um, north—"

"Ellie." Louie tried for her attention.

"Northwest," Ellie corrected herself. *Maybe she has one of those faces...*

"Ellie." Louie leaned his head back to get her attention.

"What?"

"Look."

Ellie followed his finger as he pointed across the fire.

On the other side, a woman stood with a medium-sized black dog. All Ellie could see of the woman was a lovely light-red dress and silvery, long hair that ran down the full length of the woman's back. She couldn't hear the woman's voice, but it seemed like she had the other half completely engulfed in a story.

Before the mysterious woman, images made from the sand swirl and reform through a well-coordinated dance. The dog between her knees ducked, rolled, and turned with the story. They were like mystical, beautifully choreographed dancers.

"That's amazing," Ellie admired.

"That's Kiki and her dog, Moon Bear; they always put on a little show," their neighbor explained.

"Is it a Familiar?" Ellie asked.

"No, but not your average dog." As if by some odd twist of life, Mitsy happened to bark at this moment. "No offense, Mits. It's definitely some sort of creature we know nothing about. When any of us ask, Kiki just says he's a part of her, like part of her spirit, her soul."

"Wouldn't that be a soulmate?" Ellie countered.

"Soulmates don't only come as a Familiar." Her neighbor sat back. "Some of us are lucky enough to find ours in other ways."

"What's that, honey?" The man beside her turned to look at her. He had a beautiful, friendly smile, kind eyes behind glasses, dark skin, and thick black hair.

"Shut up and kiss me." She chuckled.

"Yes, ma'am."

Ellie turned away to give them a moment of privacy and returned her attention to the show. The woman spun around as a thick swirl of sand followed and dissipated behind her with glamorous discipline. With a definitive flourish, the performer threw her hand in the air, and half of the circle erupted in applause. The story, the show, was over.

"Woo!" Ellie cheered.

A gentle wind rolled up the beach. A deep bow from Kiki and her dog signified their departure. On the gust of wind, their bodies dematerialized like a rapidly eroded rockface. They soared away in fine particles of sand.

"I'm amazed by her control," Ellie muttered. "How do you even begin learning to do all that?"

"By taking a brave leap," the man chimed in from her left.

"Or trusting fate?" her neighbor added with a smile, as if it was some inside joke.

"I guess so. The magic calls to you," Ellie added. "Or it plummets through the sky into a cake like a boulder."

Louie tilted his head back into her lap, a wide smile across his face. "I would have been more graceful if I wasn't kicked."

Her neighbor laughed into her drink and had to pull away from it so it didn't come out her nose. "That sounds like a good story. You have to tell me what happened."

Ellie couldn't help herself. This time, *she* would tell this story. "Alright, alright. So, it was my Becoming Ceremony, right? I'm up there in this hideous, old-fashioned dress—"

"A dirndl," her neighbor added.

"Yes! That's what my Mee-Maw calls it, at least."

"What color was yours?"

"Green, and of course, it was a hand-me-down. I guess it was my Aunt Kelly's dress, too."

Her neighbor's smile widened into a grin that suggested she knew something Ellie didn't.

"What?" Ellie pushed.

"Nothing. I just know hand-me-downs. Mother was a tight-fisted woman, so everything was hand-me-downs in our house." She gestured for Ellie to continue with her story. "Sorry, continue."

"Okay, so I go up to show everyone what I can do—which is not like… what Kiki can do."

"I like it," Louie countered.

"You are biased. I can make static electricity with my hands. Like, whoop-de-do."

"That's cool." Her neighbor smiled.

"Thank you. I didn't think so at the time. I was nervous, embarrassed, everything. So, I bow my head, and my Mee-Maw kisses and blows out the candle. Then, we finish off with the family members, and the other guests are about to come up when my cousin Lianne shouts, 'Look out!' And from the sky, this fire ball comes rushing forward—"

Louie made a whistling sound and formed a fist, mimicking a ball as it dropped down to Earth. When he reached Mitsy, his mouth mocked an explosion, and a playful belly rub ensued.

"Boom!" Ellie interjected. "Right into the center of the table—and my Mee-Maw's pride and joy, her—"

"Double-chocolate, raspberry layered cake?" her neighbor cut in.

"Yeah!" Ellie's smile grew. "Wait, how'd you know?"

"Because Pamela Keller-Wagner is a one-trick pony with a stick up her ass."

"That's so true!" Ellie's cheeks hurt from smiling so much. Nobody aside from her father had the bravery to say anything negative about her grandmother.

The smile remained on Ellie's face as she shoved another piece of food into her mouth. She was part of the way through her mastication when she stopped chewing.

"Wait, how do you know who my Mee-Maw is? I never said it."

The woman's knowing smile only grew.

"How?" Ellie pushed, and her own smile started to fade.

"Your name's Ellie, right?"

She nodded.

"Your mom's Kimberly?"

Again, Ellie nodded and double-checked the woman's attire. The stranger wasn't a person her father warned her about.

"You know your Aunt Kelly has a twin, right?"

"Yeah, but she ran away when she was—"

"Seventeen." The stranger leaned over her armchair. "I'm so happy to finally get to meet you."

22

Corruption

"I, uh, I know that the family can be really strict, and they've probably said some terrible things about me. I... uh... I'm not springing this on you to have a relationship or anything." The smile faded from Jean's face as she tried to explain herself. "I just wanted to be forward and let you know who I am."

"This is so cool," Ellie said breathlessly before she tapped Louie's shoulder rapidly. "Louie!"

"Yes?" Louie lifted up Mitsy and pretended to have her speak on his behalf. The dog did not look enthused.

"This is serious." Ellie tried to hide her laughter. "This is Jean! My aunt Jean!"

"Kelly's sister?" Louie put down Mitsy and turned around completely to look at the two of them. "Ah... I see it now."

Jean sat back calmly. She held Louie in her gaze and lifted one eyebrow.

"You're the prettier twin," he reassured her.

Jean smiled wide and tipped her beer to him. "I like him. He's smart."

"So, did you do it?" Ellie asked excitedly. "Did you marry the werewolf?"

"I understand the concern." Jean's husband leaned forward. "People think I'm just going to rip them apart—not the case."

Before he could finish explaining, Louie managed to put himself between Ellie and the werewolf.

He chuckled. "It's okay. The moon has its weakest pull on me right now," he explained. "And I sequester myself to a small island off of the bay on a full moon."

"Our system has worked for more than thirty years without incident," Jean added. "Peter has it all under control."

"I'm Peter, by the way." Her husband gave a quick wave.

As they exchanged quick pleasantries, Louie's shoulders relaxed, but he didn't move from his protective stance.

"Besides, it's not like the Wagner's description," Jean continued. "Our ancestor condemned werewolves, but Peter's not mindless and rabid."

Peter rolled his eyes.

"Sorry, babe. I know you don't like that word." Jean affectionately squeezed his knee.

Peter said nothing.

"Anyway, Peter just has a shorter fuse. If he doesn't like you, well, then he *really* doesn't like you. I mean, let's be logical. At the core of all dogs, aren't they pack creatures? Werewolves were never meant to be these rogue animals that roam the countryside. They're pack animals."

"And now the teacher's side comes out," Peter teased. "This isn't about me; get to know our niece."

Jean exchanged a thoughtful look with Peter before she adjusted in her seat and turned her attention back to Ellie and Louie.

"Sorry. I teach at the school here twice a week. He's right, though. Tell me about yourself."

Ellie chuckled awkwardly. "Man, I, uh, hate talking about myself."

"Of course, teenage girl." Jean shook her head. "My daughter, Grace, is thirteen, and getting her to talk about herself is like pulling teeth."

"I have a cousin?"

"You have four, actually." Jean leaned back in her chair and pointed toward a smaller fire where a young man stood and helped children put marshmallows on sticks. It was hard to make out details in the limited light. "That's our oldest, Tristan; he's helping the kids with s'mores. Brody and Michael are the ones fighting with their—Boys!"

Ellie could see two young boys; one was around the age of ten, the other a few years younger. They fought with marshmallow sticks like they were swords. The tips of their sticks were on fire with molten sugar.

"Stop! There's fire on—Thank you, Tristan."

Jean turned back towards the fire and exhaled exasperatedly. Her eyes grew wide as she looked at her husband with a hand held up. "I have no idea how they make it through the day without accidentally killing themselves."

Peter kissed her on the cheek and stood from his chair. "I'll talk to them."

"Thank you, babe!"

Peter disappeared in the darkness but reappeared in the light of the other fire. He knelt to the boys' level and spoke to them as they held their sticks.

"We say the gods blessed us with Tristan at a young age because they knew we could handle him. Grace was our princess and was brought to us when we needed her most. The boys, well, they were both 'surprises.' The gods must have figured that no matter how old we got, we would never be prepared for them, so might as well."

Ellie chuckled.

"He's a good dad," Jean continued. "I don't regret running off with him. I mean, I miss my sisters, my father."

Oh no, she doesn't know about grandpa. Ellie's heart sank into her stomach.

"But if I had stayed, I would've been forced to marry that Gagnon boy, and I wouldn't have all of this." Jean gestured to the area around them. "Not to say—this isn't my house. We live in Wellfleet. But you get what I'm saying?"

"Yeah, I get it." A tinge of guilt pierced Ellie's stomach. "Ever think about going back?"

Jean grimaced and shook her head slightly. "Ellie, when you leave, you can never go back."

Ellie straightened up. She looked at Louie, then her aunt.

"Yeah, you didn't know?" Jean explained. "When you leave, you're disowned. Mother always threatened that I'd be Guided, but I think that's just a myth parents tell their kids to keep them in line."

Ellie shook her head from side to side. "No? No. Disowned means you're like... cut off. You're dead to them. Right?"

"Yeah." Jean nodded.

"My dad and I still talk."

"Yeah," Louie added. "He gave her a motorcycle and a cell phone before we left."

Jean's expression didn't soften as she tried to process that information. "I'm sorry, Ellie. I thought you knew... I'd love to hear about how you left."

Elated over the invitation, Ellie leaned over the armrest to tell her aunt about the lasagna night, the journals, and everything that came before her departure. As the evening progressed, Ellie and Jean moved their conversation from the fireside to the beach. Jean kept an eye on the clock and explained that at midnight, they would convene around the tiki torches and bring forth a Calling Circle.

"A Calling Circle?" Ellie looked at Louie with concerned eyes. "For what?"

"To thank our Seers and to make offerings to the Void." Jean shrugged happily. "It's really popular in magical communities."

"Oh, cool!" Louie exclaimed. "If it's a full calling circle, I could say hey to Betty."

"Betty? As in Betty Fischer? She's our Seer?" Jean leaned in towards Louie with excitement.

"Yeah, she's great."

"You think she'll have some feelings about you stealing her journal?" Jean asked Ellie.

"I hope not!" Ellie playfully grimaced.

"I bet Kimmy's losing her mind over you stealing it—and for leaving. Oh man, even as a kid, she was anal-retentive."

The sands beneath their feet shimmered against the star-lit sky. The murmur of the party was still behind them as their walk slowed to a saunter.

"Oh! Look!" Louie had stopped about ten feet behind them and gestured to a shooting star in the sky. "You got this, buddy!"

Ellie looked up, expecting to catch the tail end of it, but it was long gone.

"I bet they made it," Louie said with the biggest smile on his face.

Beneath the starlight, with the backdrop of the dark cape, Louie was the most beautiful person Ellie had ever seen. Her gaze softened as she took in the view.

"Hee hee." Jean playfully nudged Ellie's shoulder.

"Stop." Ellie playfully shushed her.

"You see a shooting star, Lou?" Jean asked.

"Not a shooting star—a Familiar," he called back. "It's that time. I can feel it." Louie brought a thoughtful hand to his stomach.

"Feel it?" Ellie questioned softly.

"Yeah," Jean said. "Familiars can—"

Just then, a twig snapped in the sand dunes along the edge of the beach. Louie hurried to Ellie's side and put a protective shoulder between her and the mysterious snap. After a second, Jean didn't seem concerned, but Louie stayed vigilant.

"What is it?" Ellie asked and kept her eyes ahead.

"Something," Louie muttered thoughtfully as his eyes scanned the sand dunes. "Just wait a second."

There was a rustle of branches and a sudden smash against the sand ten meters in front of them, followed by a rustle of screeches.

"Owl," Louie informed her quietly. "Got a squirrel."

"Ah, man. That would've been cool to see," Ellie said.

"No." Louie's voice was flat. "It's not cute. You'd be upset."

"Oh." Ellie looked away from the scene before she could accidentally see anything.

"They're gone," Louie informed her, and a comforting hand rubbed Ellie's lower back. She turned to face Louie.

Amongst the rolling waves, the twinkling stars above, and his beautiful eyes dancing in the glimmering lights, Ellie felt her heart shudder with excitement. "So, kind of you to protect me from the owl."

"Always. Owls, bees, anything."

Without thinking, Ellie stood on her tippy toes and gently kissed Louie's cheek.

A wide smile brightened his face. "You haven't given me a kiss since I changed."

Ellie reached behind her back and gently took his hand. "Told you I just need some time."

"We should probably head back." Jean glanced at her watch. "Don't want to miss your first Calling Circle... I hope the boys aren't giving Peter too much trouble."

"It would be pretty cool to meet this famous Seer." Ellie and Louie turned back toward the party, hand-in-hand.

Louie didn't move with her, though. Ellie looked back to see his eyes locked back on the spot the owl emerged from.

"C'mon, they may have leftover meatballs." Ellie beckoned him and gave him a second tug, but he remained firmly in place, scanning the terrain.

Suddenly, Louie whipped around and looked up towards the sky. "Move!" He shoved Ellie hard, knocking her to the wet ground, just as a thick darkness, unlike anything this world could produce, crashed between the two of them.

"Louie? What was that?" Ellie called out, no longer at his side.

"Jean!" Peter's once-kind voice was now a deep, threatening growl.

"Peter?" Jean called out.

The hunched, bipedal figure darted up the beach at an impossible, inhuman speed.

"Somethings wrong! Something's here. I can hear it," Peter roared. A rough, hot exhale left his snarling face and bright-white sharp teeth. "Find Gracey. Protect the boys," Peter ordered. "Take Ellie and run."

A trail of burning, black tar marked the sand, creating a wall between Ellie and Louie. Ellie heard a guttural gargling call, which resonated in her chest before it compounded rapidly into an ear-piercing screech that made Ellie flinch.

Louie stood beyond the flames, his shoulders crouched down with a deadly look on his face.

A creature of darkness. Those damn words haunted Ellie. *Ellie-Lynne Betty Becker will meet her fate one spring eve.*

"This is it!" She gasped. "Louie! This is it—the prophecy," she yelled.

Pain echoed inside her as the creature from her nightmares turned and faced her. Just like her dream, there were no eyes, but she could feel its gaze, its desperation. Pitch-black drops, as thick as molasses, dripped like syrupy goo as it opened its mouth and let out another shriek.

"Ellie, get back." Someone grabbed her foot and yanked her away from the fire towards the party. She looked back over her shoulder to see her uncle stalking toward the creature.

"No! You can't," Ellie tried to warn him.

That cry sounded again, and Ellie shivered, paralyzed in her place. The creature kept its attention focused on her and took a step in her direction. The mouth moved as if it was trying to form words, but it only gargled nonsense. Suddenly, the creature evolved before her eyes, and its mouth became more defined. A booming, hollow "Mine" erupted from its lips.

"I don't think so." Her uncle, who had transformed into a large, hairy beast, stood in the sand before her, blocking her path.

The glow of a raging fire lit up the sandy beach. The familiar molten mass stepped forward and sparked before her. He rushed forward and wrapped his arms around the oozing beast.

"Louie, no!" Ellie yelled.

Louie sizzled and popped as the slow, syrupy creature turned its attention to him. The blackness tried to overtake and encompass him, but with one fluid motion, Louie and his foe shot toward the starry sky. The force of Louie's burst of speed rippled through the air and knocked Peter on top of Ellie.

"Are you okay?" The werewolf snarled as he jumped up and offered a hairy, disfigured hand to Ellie.

Where the creature had stood, a thick line of black sludge dissipated beneath the smoldering flames Louie left in his wake. Ellie's eyes followed the trajectory of the blast into the sky. A light twinkled off in the distance.

"Louie?"

23

Poison

Not this time," Louie promised as he jetted towards a tear in the night sky that offered an entrance into the Void. "It took me fourteen years to be with her! You're not taking her from me!"

Louie struggled to hold on to his viscous foe, and each time he made an adjustment, his fiery core waned.

She's going to be all alone down there. He tightened his grip. *Who will protect her from bees? Check under the bed when she watches a scary movie?*

Louie couldn't bring himself to glance down to the Earth below them—to the beach where he left her on the ground. He couldn't allow his last image of her being terrified, helpless, and on her back in the sand.

I can't die, not tonight. She's such a gentle soul. I don't want the world to hurt her more.

The tent, alone in those woods, plagued his mind.

She can't sleep there alone.

The Corrupted Familiar struggled in his arms. Louie knew this creature had been driven mad by loneliness, so he wasn't surprised when it oozed a contagious plague that threatened to poison Louie's mind.

The Corrupted Familiar's gnarly teeth sunk into his shoulder, and its plague spread through the venom of its bite. Heartache, dread, and loneliness seeped through Louie's shoulder, mercilessly spreading like webbing up his neck.

"*She never loved you.*"

"*Worthless dog.*"

Louie tried to shake away the thoughts. He *had* to focus and fight the poison feeding him lies. *Don't give in.*

"*You held her back.*"

"*She can't look at you.*"

"No!" Louie whimpered as his confidence faltered. He took a deep breath. He knew he had to keep his fire bright and lit, or he could burn out. *Hold on. Hold on for her.* He couldn't release the Corrupted Familiar until they were in The Void, or it would find its way back to Ellie, so Louie took each bite like a punch to the face.

"*Useless.*"

"*Pathetic.*"

"Stop it," Louie wailed, and with a burst from his fiery core, he sent a rush of flames over them both. "Stop!"

Just like the night he began his journey to Ellie, a crisp tear in the night sky, invisible to the human eye, welcomed the Familiars, but tonight, Louie struggled and fought as they raced towards the Corruption's prison cell.

Through the entrance, the endless cosmos above decorated the sky as Louie entered The Void with all the grace and precision as before—screaming headfirst, and at full speed. Only this time, Louie was determined not to crash into a rock. He turned their bodies so the Corrupted Familiar braced his fall and took the full force of the impact against the faltered, broken ground.

As sadness, doubt, and self-hate feasted on Louie's kind mind, Louie surveyed the end result of this infection—a creature with the substance as partially digested jello, the speed of a bullet, and the strength of a rabid elephant.

Its movements were slow compared to Louie's. With a burst of speed that hit like a cannonball, Louie rushed the creature. Hit after hit, explosions of fire and sparks filled the darkness around them, but he was only able to do so much damage, as the infected parts of his body grew limp and heavy. His molten core slowed, but he rammed himself again and again like a battering ram against his foe.

I can't keep this up, Louie thought as he felt the cold taint his core. "Seer! Seer, please! I have to stop it," he cried out through the limitless expanse.

As Louie lost momentum and strength, the once-slow threat seemed more ominous as its untiring teeth approached.

I love you, Ellie. A whimper left Louie's lips as another bite sunk into him, and his last bit of sparks faded. "Betty, please!"

"Mmmmmhmmm." It was distant at first. "Mmmhmm-hmmmm."

The familiar, jazzy tune compounded and rushed forth through the darkness.

"Thank the Void," Louie uttered as the bizarre and beautiful orchestra rushed upon the battle.

Louie saw an eccentric wispy form with oblong shimmering silver eyes bound toward them—only, it wasn't alone. A sea of glistening reflective orbs rushed forward as dozens of Seers responded to Louie's call. Their feathery bodies merged into one powerful being and crashed into the unwanted foe. Quickly, like sprinkles of sand in the wind, the Corrupted Familiar dematerialized into nothingness.

Louie struggled to keep his core together as he regressed to his shooting star form—a meager liquified rock. Words eluded him, and he only managed to spout a little puff of gas.

Betty Fischer scooped him up and held him close. Louie looked up to his dear friend, Betty, thankful they were reunited. The last time they were together, they walked hand in hand to find her great, great, great, grand niece's puddle. Now, she carried him lovingly.

The group of Seers escorted them and stoked Louie's fiery center with bits of rocks. Still holding Louie, Betty plunged her wispy free hand into her misty form to her hard, condensed center. She fiddled around, and with a snap, she pulled out a bit of her organic body to fuel Louie.

Finally, Ellie's comforting, familiar pool shimmered in the distance. Betty placed Louie down along the bank of the pool.

Down below, beyond Louie's reach, Ellie wailed louder and harder than she had when she first entered the world nineteen years ago. Crumpled in a heap of misery on her knees in the sand, she howled, looking at the sky. Jean wrapped her arms around her niece, comforting her.

Ellie, I promise, I will get strong enough to come back to you.

Thank You!

There's still so much more to tell...

Have you ever wondered what a Familiar has to go through to find their witch or wizard and why so few exist?

Scan the QR code below to sign up for my newsletter and get exclusive content, such as Little Star's Journey, character art, and more!